A Night at the Opera

The Mysteries of Stickleback Hollow®

By C.S. Woolley

A Mightier Than the Sword UK Publication

©2023

A Night at the Opera

The Mysteries of Stickleback Hollow®

By C. S. Woolley

A Mightier Than the Sword UK Publication

Paperback Edition

ISBN Paperback 978-1-99-117086-6

ISBN Hardback 978-1-99-117087-3

ISBN Kindle 978-1-7386037-6-3

Copyright © c. s. woolley 2023

Cover Design © c. s. woolley 2023

The Mysteries of Stickleback Hollow® is a Registered Trademark 1235153

For

Roger

Author's Note

Thanks for taking the time to read A Night at the Opera, this particular book is one that is very special to me. My friend, Roger, to whom this book is dedicated, has been experiencing a rather difficult time and, in order to help him, a trilogy of novella collections was born and created.

This story has been created solely for one of the collections on limited release. After that release, it will be available as a novella raising money for homeless charities.

So if you are reading this, thank you for helping to support the tireless work of so many in keeping people from losing their homes and being forced to live on the street. It is a situation that so many are far closer to than we realise and the immense pressure it puts on your health and mental well-being is far

greater than I could ever accurately describe.

In the course of this story, multiple languages are spoken. For the longer speeches, I have left the language in English to allow the reading experience not to be impeded, but for the shorter pieces or where characters switch between English and another language the other language remains. The translations for both the English speeches in other languages and the other languages that remain in the text can be found translated at the back of the book before the Historical Note.

Kia Kaha.

The Characters

Lady Sarah Montgomery Baird Watson-Wentworth

The heroine

Mr Alexander Hunter Webb-Kneelingroach

A huntsman and heir to Grangeback Estate

Constable Arwyn Evans

Policeman in Stickleback Hollow

Sylvia

Lady Sarah's Companion and Lady's Maid.

Pattinson

An Akita, Alexander's hunting dog

Stanley & Lee Baker

Sons of Miss Baker

Brigadier George Webb-Kneelingroach

Lord of Grangeback, Father of Alexander, and Lady Sarah's Guardian

Bosworth

The butler

Mrs Bosworth

The housekeeper

Cooky

The cook

Mr Thomas Egerton

Son of Wilbraham & Elizabeth

Mr Edward Christopher Egerton

Son of Wilbraham & Elizabeth

Mr Oliver Henry Brown

An American Gentleman, Cousin to the Egerton Family

Signorina Aurora Ricci

Prima Donna Soprano

Mr Ernest Boult

Stage Manager at Covent Garden

Señor Julio Mendez

Internationally Renown Violinist

Herr Bruno Wagner

A Conductor

Mr Hector Jamieson

An Actor

Monsieur Jacques Lavingne

Theatre Manger of Covent Garden

Signorina Isabella Ricci

Deceased twin of Aurora

March 1841

Chapter 1

Music, an element of expression, once it takes

hold of you shall live in your soul forever. At least that was

how lady Cynthia Watson Wentworth had always described

it to her daughter. There was nothing that delighted her more

than music.

When Sarah was a child, her mother had filled their

home in India with music and since her mother's death, it

was the absence of music that made her feel the loss most

keenly.

Grangeback Manor was not a silent bastion

overlooking Stickleback Hollow, but it was only filled with

music at parties, or when Lady Sarah provided it.

In India, her mother had a cadre of musicians to

perform all manner of music that shifted with whatever mood

Lady Cynthia was seized by.

She had ensured her daughter had been given full instruction on the piano, cello, harp, and violin. But even though playing music reminded Lady Sarah of her parents, and brought her mother closer, it was not the same as when the musicians had played in her childhood.

She had been living at Grangeback Manor for several years and only once had she been seen any form of musical performance.

At parties there were musicians playing waltzes, and providing a quiet background ambience, but there had been only one concert where the music had been the sole focus of her attention.

When she first arrived in England, her relatives had taken her to a salon to hear some third rate musicians stumble their way through Rachmaninov. It had been a disappointing evening that Lady Sarah had not been keen to repeat.

But as time had slipped by, it become apparent that as disappointing and unrewarding a night of poorly played music was, it was better than no music at all.

After dinner one evening when the halls should have resounded with sound, Lady Sarah found that she can no longer bear such a quiet world.

"Brigadier," she announced suddenly, breaking the silence in the library. "I have a request."

Brigadier George Webb-Kneelingroach, Lord of Grangeback, and guardian of Lady Sarah had been dozing off by the fire quite contentedly after a rather good meal. The sound of Lady Sara's voice had woken him shortly and caused his son, Mr Alexander Hunter Webb-Kneelingroach, to snicker.

"What is it, my dear girl?" George asked as he cast a dark look in the direction of Alex.

"I would like to go to a musical performance," Lady Sara replied firmly and waited to receive protests that would that would require overcoming before such an outing could be arranged.

"What a capital idea, Hunter, what say you to such an excursion?" the Brigadier said with delight.

"Her leadership's wishes my command," Alex replied warmly. Hunter was his mother's name and he was a bastard he had been recognised by his father as his son and co-heir of grade back along with Lady Sarah.

It was an unusual situation. But as the two were to marry, the lawyers had agreed the standing did no harm. But Mr. Hunter had been unwilling to part with his mother's name, and so had been arranged that not only would he be allowed to keep her name, his father would refer to him as such in private as well as in public.

"I'm most happy to hear you're both so eager for such an evening," Lady Sarah smiled.

"It has been far too long since I was last at Covent Garden, that is of course the only place that we can ensure that you have the most wonderful evening," the brigadier mused as he rubbed his chin. "You've never been to Covent

Garden, have you my dear? Well, I dare say we shall find some entertainment there. Mrs Bosworth!" the brigadier yelled.

A few moments later, Mrs Bosworth, the housekeeper, entered the room with a look of thunder on her face. She had worked for the brigadier for many years, but she was not accustomed to be simply yelled for like a dog.

"Can I help, brigadier?" Mrs Bosworth asked through gritted teeth.

"Ah, Mrs Bosworth, what was the name of that opera singer who is performing at Covent Garden? I was reading about it in the paper a few days ago," George asked with a wave of his hand.

"I am sorry, brigadier, I do not know what you were reading over breakfast," Mrs Bosworth replied with a slight look of disbelief on her face.

Lady Sarah and Alex shared an amused glance and did their best to stifle laughter that threatened to escape from their lips.

"Of course you do, it was the woman that everyone has been praising recently. The singer with the voice," the brigadier said with a slight frown.

"Sir, you may have spoken to someone about it over breakfast, but you did not speak to me about it. Perhaps you should speak to Sylvia about it when she returns from her evening with the constable," Mrs Bosworth said, with an irritated edge to her voice.

"Ah yes, it must have been Sylvia I spoke to. Well then, perhaps you might be so kind to find me the newspaper with the concert listing in," George said with a wave of his hand.

"Very well, sir," Mrs Bosworth said sourly and went to search through the stack of newspapers in the kitchen that were awaiting use as kindling for the fires.

Though the great manor house had lands full of trees where kindling could be gathered, on wet days and winter nights where the snow was thick on the ground, the newspapers were used as a substitute.

Sylvia was Lady Sarah's companion and personal maid, though she was treated more as a friend and confidant than an employee. She dined with the rest of the household as general rule, but this evening she had been to visit with Constable Evans in the village.

It had been a rare evening of private dining for the brigadier, Lady Sarah and Mr Hunter. Without Sylvia there, it seemed almost too quiet, but it was also unusual for Grangeback to not have guests there for dinner. The change in their routine was welcomed by the three of them, and they had very much enjoyed the more peaceful dining experience.

"I suspect Mrs Bosworth maybe some time trying to find such a needle in a haystack," Lady Sarah smirked at the brigadier.

"Well, that can't be helped. She'll find the name of the woman, I am sure. Now, Covent Garden. It is such a fine musical hall, I am surprised that your relatives in London did not take you whilst you were staying with them," the brigadier said as he rubbed his chin.

"I fear that my relatives were more interested in being seen than what they heard," Lady Sarah quipped as she shifted uncomfortably on the settee.

"Quite, so, there are many within London society for whom that is true, but I am glad to say that we are above such things," the brigadier said brightly. "As we are to go so far south, we shall need to find rooms for a day or two. I am sure that we'll be able to find accommodation close to Covent Garden, and enjoy quite the evening out. We also need to find somewhere to dine before going the performance," the brigadier said.

"I feel that wherever you choose for us to eat will be more than adequate," Mr Hunter said with a gleam in his eye.

"Now now, boy, there's no need to take that tone," the brigadier chided his son. "It would be much more agreeable if we were all to sit down and discuss the merits of a great many places that offer a variety of meals. After all, a very heavy meal before the opera could be tantamount to disaster in some situations."

"Surely it would depend on whether we went to a matinee or an evening performance," Lady Sarah pointed out.

"Ah yes, of course there is always the matinee. Take in the sights of London during the morning, the opera in the afternoon and then an evening out at dinner. That sounds like a capital idea," the brigadier said as he slapped his hand down upon the arm of his chair. "I will have Bosworth make the arrangements at once."

Without a moments hesitation, the brigadier was on his feet and walking over to the bell rope that stood by the fireplace. He pulled on it and a few moments later, footsteps could be heard in the hallway.

Bosworth, the butler, appeared with Mrs Bosworth at his shoulder looking even more peeved than she had before.

Lady Sarah was certain that her annoyance was due to Bosworth being summoned by the use of the bell rather than being yelled for like some scullery maid when she had not been afforded the same courtesy.

"Bosworth, we need you to make some arrangements for a trip to London for the three of us, and most likely Sylvia as well. I cannot see her wishing to miss out on such an occasion. We all require tickets to the soprano that Mrs Bosworth was discovering the name of, a nights accommodation, and some sort of meal at one of the finest establishments. Perhaps the Ritz would be ideal for this," the brigadier mused.

"And what date did sir have in mind?" Bosworth asked dryly.

"Ah well, this is Bosworth. Did you have any success in finding the name of the soprano?"

"I did, brigadier," Mrs Bosworth said with a slight huff in her voice. "She will be performing on the 26th, not much time at all."

"There you are, the 26th, and be sure that these arrangements are made us as quickly as possible," the brigadier instructed.

"Very well, sir. I will make my inquiries. Though I do not expect a reply to any telegram sent at this time of night until the morning," Bosworth said.

"Of course. Well, better to get started now than to wait forever," the brigadier said jovially.

The idea of such an outing had clearly buoyed his spirits, and he walked around the library wringing his hands together is a boyish excitement that was rarely seen in a man of his age.

"Will that be all, sir?" Bosworth asked.

"Oh, yes. Great. Great. Good night to both. We shall see you in the morning," the brigadier said, clearly distracted by thoughts of the excursion he was planning.

Lady Sarah cast Mrs. Bosworth an apologetic look. But

it did little to help soothe the housekeeper's ruffled feathers.

"You should be far kinder to Mrs. Bosworth than you are," Lady Sarah said with a sigh after the had closed the door behind the departing staff.

"Oh, she is a good sport. She will have forgotten any slight by tomorrow morning," the brigadier said with a wave of his hand.

"I am not sure that's entirely true, father, but I am sure she will forgive you in time," Mr Hunter said, trying not to laugh. Since his engagement to Lady Sarah had been made public, he had far more jovial than ever before and seemed to finally have settled in to his role as the heir to the manor and the estate.

"Now we must begin packing as, well, packing must be done," George said as he ignored his son's comments.

"Father, it is not until the 26th! We have ample time to pack and prepare," Alex said trying to rein in his father's excitement. "Perhaps we should sit and enjoy the fire, and maybe a game of whist?"

"Oh, not whist, bridge! Bridge is the perfect game for us to play, maybe Sarah can observe as we play a hand or two," the brigadier said.

"Or perhaps Sarah could play against the two of us. If we cannot play with four hands, then we will be playing whist," Alex sighed and cast an amused glance at his betrothed.

"Blast it all," the brigadier cried with disappointment.

"Sylvia will be back soon, no doubt. We can play bridge when she returns. Until then, we will simply have to enjoy the fire," Lady Sarah said comfortingly.

"Perhaps music would be in order whilst we wait, my dear," the Brigadier said with a smile.

"How could I refuse such a request?" Sarah smiled and arose from the settee upon which she had sat with Mr Hunter, and moved to the grand piano that stood in the corner of the library.

"Do we have any requests gentleman?" Lady Sarah asked as she settled herself on the piano stool.

"I think a sonata would be quite wonderful this evening, whichever one comes to mind," the brigadier said.

There were piles of sheet music for the piano that had been collected over the years from various locations around the world. Some of it the brigadier had come across in his travels.

Others had been sent to his late wife who was also a great lover of music, though she rarely played.   Other pieces had simply been left behind by musicians who had been performing at one grand event or another in the manor.

Lady Sarah lifted the lid on the piano and rooted around amongst the piles of music until she found a piece that she enjoyed playing.

As the night drifted on, music filled the halls of Grangeback. The kitchen staff listened with smiles on their faces as they finished cleaning up after the evening meal and made their way to their beds. Cooky, as always, was the last to turn in.

"Oh, Mrs. Bosworth. It's so nice to hear the piano being played," Cooky said to the housekeeper as the two made their final rounds of the great house.

"It is indeed, Cooky. Such a shame that the brigadier is becoming far more priggish in his old age when he has so much he should be thankful for," Mrs Bosworth said dryly.

"What do we expect from a man such as he?" Cooky replied with a smile, "He is revelling in his own good fortunate and forgetting those that have been loyal to him through these harder years. I am sure he will apologise in the morning."

"I am sure he will not, Cooky, but I suppose I will have to get forgive him regardless."

The two women shuffled around the house, making sure all was as it should be. Bosworth would remain awake until Sylvia returned to the house before he would lock a door and retire to his bed.

Satisfied that everything was in its place and that no ill would befall the household that night, the two women said their goodnights and went to their beds.

When Silvia eventually did return to the house, she was as eager as the others had been for the trip to London and an afternoon of Opera. The four played bridge well into the early hours of the morning, discussing all that they would accomplish on their trip to the capital.

The telegram to Covent Garden was sent with all alacrity by Bosworth but he did not send the telegram to the Ritz regarding the diner and accommodation arrangements. The butler knew better than to assume that tickets would be readily available for such a performance.

It wasn't until the following day at 3 o'clock in the afternoon that a reply to the telegram was received from Covent Garden.

The telegram was short and to the point.

"Sold out"

The news was delivered to the brigadier, Lady Sarah, Sylvia and Mr Hunter separately.

Mr Hunter was the least disappointed about not having to trek all the way to London for a musical performance, but he still felt a pang at the thought of the missed opportunity.

Though Sylvia merely shrugged off the news with a nonchalant "Never mind" she did her best to avoid the rest of the household for a few hours so she could hide her feelings from them.

The brigadier sank into a sudden state of melancholy and locked himself in his office in response to being deprived of the excursion he had been so diligently planning.

Lady Sarah went riding for a few hours with her Japanese hunting dog, Pattinson, at her side. The Akita was always glad to spend his time running around the grounds of Grangeback chasing after Black Guy, the Friesian stallion that her ladyship rode.

She returned to Grangeback later that evening when she had ridden away all of her upset and anger at being denied and afternoon of opera. Instead she decided to content herself with playing the piano whilst Sylvia and Mr Hunter listened.

But a serendipitous knock at the door of the manor was about to change all that.

Chapter 2

It was Mrs Bosworth who answered the door. It was not her usual practice, but as Bosworth was otherwise engaged with attending to the brigadier, she had temporarily assumed some of her husband's duties.

She was surprised to see three familiar faces stood on the doorstep.

"Mrs Bosworth, how wonderful to see you. Is the household at home to visitors?" Thomas Egerton asked as he beamed broadly at the housekeeper.

"The brigadier is currently indisposed, but the rest of the household are in the library. Perhaps you would be good enough to join them," Mrs Bosworth suggested.

The three men had visited the house often, and though it was polite and normal practice for any visitors, no matter how frequent, to be announced, Mrs Bosworth had other duties that she had to attend to.

Seeing the flustered look on her face, none of the gentlemen commented on her lapse in protocol.

"What a capital idea!" Mr Brown said, his thick American accent doing it's best to imitate the brigadier.

The cousin of the Egertons, Mr Brown had bought a house in the neighbourhood when he had been competing with Mr Hunter to win Lady Sarah's hand. But after she had chosen Mr Hunter, the brigadier had taken the young man under his wing.

The pair had spent many afternoons hunting on both their lands. The brigadier knew the sting of rejection all too well from the days before he met his wife, and he knew that it was never easy being far from your homeland when trying to make a life for yourself.

As a result, the pair had become fast friends, and Mr Brown had managed to find a way to be happy for both Mr Hunter and Lady Sarah, and support their life together as a friend.

Edward laugh as his cousin's impression of the lord of the manor, and led the way through the halls of the great house to the library.

"What ho!" he called as he opened the door to the library.

Mr Hunter was stood by the piano and smiled at seeing his friends appear, he moved away from the instrument to greet them.

Sylvia was sat embroidering a sampler on one of the chairs and did not take her eyes from it as the men entered.

Lady Sarah was so lost in the music she was playing that she did not even notice the arrival of the three men until she had finished playing.

"What a pleasant surprise," she said with a genuine smile as she rose from the piano stool. "What brings you all here this evening?"

"We come bearing an invitation. Our dear mother,

and aunt, has a very special guest visiting and she has

organised a musical salon at Tatton Park to celebrate,"

Thomas said grandly.

Mr Hunter smiled to himself and went to ring the bell.

A moment later, Mrs Bosworth appeared at the door looking

more flustered than before. Mr Hunter whispered something

to her and she vanished a few seconds later.

"And would this special guest happen to be an opera

singer? A soprano perhaps of world renown?" Mr Hunter

asked knowingly.

"Why Hunter, you devil! How did you know?"

Edward asked with surprise.

Lady Sarah laughed and related the story of their

conversation the night before and their failure to secure

tickets to see her perform.

"Well then, how serendipitous this is for us all! She

will be performing on Tuesday next week at the house before

she travels to London to make ready for her concerts at

Covent Garden," Mr Brown explained.

"Then tell your mother, aunt, that we will all be delighted to attend!" the brigadier cried with joy as he flung open the door to the library.

Mrs Bosworth could be seen in the hallway shaking her head as she went back to work. Sylvia frowned slightly and put down her sampler to go after the housekeeper.

"Is something wrong?" Sylvia asked as she cornered Mrs Bosworth in the drawing room.

"Perhaps. Do you not find the brigadier's sudden mood swings to be somewhat out of character?" Mrs Bosworth sighed as she looked at Lady Sarah's companion with concern etched on her face.

"From what people have told me of him, he has not been himself since his return from India, but I have only known him a short time. The news of Grace's death, the departure of Millie, whatever horrors he saw overseas, any number of these things could be affecting him," Sylvia replied thoughtfully.

"Do not mention any of this to the others, they have all assumed he is merely becoming more eccentric as he ages," Mrs Bosworth warned.

"Of course not, but you fear this is something far more serious?" Sylvia replied.

"I do, but without the doctor's help, I cannot know anything for certain," Mrs Bosworth sighed a second time.

"Then when the doctor returns, we shall go and visit with him," Sylvia said comfortingly.

"He and the reverend should be back any day now. I am not sure why two men of such advanced aged decided that a walking holiday in the Lakes was a good idea, but they will be home soon," Mrs Bosworth said with a small measure of relief.

Chapter
3

Tuesday soon rolled around, and though the doctor

had returned from his walking holiday, there had not been a

moment that Mrs Bosworth and Sylvia could find to go and

visit with him when the brigadier would not notice their

absence.

Excitement had filled the atmosphere at the manor

house, and it was due in no small part to the brigadier's own

giddy anticipation of seeing the soprano perform.

Lady Sarah had a new dress that Miss Angela Baker,

the village dressmaker and seamstress had created for the

occasion, as did Sylvia. They were brought to the manor by

Lee and Stanley Baker, her adopted sons, who had both been

keen to visit the great house again.

Miss Baker had been one of the party that had

travelled to India with the brigadier in the service of the

crown, and in her absence, the twins had been in the

guardianship of Lady Sarah and had lived at Grangeback.

Their time around her ladyship had convinced them

both that they wanted to solve mysteries for a living, but their

mother had insisted that they find a master to be apprenticed

to.

Cooky was pleased to see the boys and spoilt them

with treats she had baked and told them to come back and see

her the next day for more. Pattinson had also been glad to see

his two playmates and the three had raced around the house,

darting through secret passages and causing Mrs Bosworth

no small amount of heart attacks.

Mr Hunter and the brigadier dressed in their best

evening coats for the occasion, each with a waistcoat that had

been fashioned to match the fabric of Lady Sarah's and

Sylvia's dresses.

The carriage was summoned when the two ladies

were ready, and Lee and Stanley Baker begged to be allowed

to join the party. The brigadier was resistant to the idea at first, but Mrs Bosworth brought out the suits that had been made for the two boys last Christmas and George soon relented.

The boys changed with far more speed than anyone thought possible and were racing out the door to climb into the carriage before anyone could stop them.

The journey to Tatton Park was not long, but neither was it short, and by the time they arrived, the brigadier was glad for the chance to disembark and walk around in the cool night air.

Mrs Egerton was thrilled to see her guests dressed in their finery and both Charlotte and Charles, the youngest of the Egerton children, were equally thrilled to see their partners-in-crime had also come along.

The four children had caused all sorts of mischief during the Christmas celebrations at Grangeback, and had sent secret letters to each other ever since.

Upon greeting each other, the four promptly vanished.

"Those children will be the death of me," Mrs Egerton sighed and shook her head.

"Oh dear Elizabeth, they are good at heart. I am sure that they will find their own entertainment this evening and do nothing to disrupt us," Lady Sarah said affectionately.

"I suppose you are right, now come, you must meet with our special guest," Elizabeth sighed and immediately brightened as she escorted her guests into the house.

The salon was being held in the ballroom of the great house. The high ceilings provided excellent acoustics for musical performances and there was space for dancing, should it prove to be appropriate.

The other guests were limited to the Egertons and Mr Brown, so it was an intimate affair that did not require any stiff and uncomfortable conversation.

"May I present Signorina Aurora Ricci, direct from

The Teatro di San Carlo in Naples. She is an old friend of the family and it is our great honour to have her here before she travels to London for her performances next week," Elizabeth Egerton said with grandeur as she presented the soprano to her guests.

"What a pleasure. Non vedo l'ora di sentirti cantare. Ho sentito molte cose su di te," Lady Sarah said as she and the opera singer stood face-to-face.

"Oh che meraviglia ascoltare la mia lingua qui. But I have promised to speak as much English as I can whilst in your country. Ma tu hai un bel cuore. Fare un gesto del genere mi ha fatto sentire un po' meno la mancanza della mia patria," Aurora said warmly and hugged Lady Sarah tightly.

There was a short period of milling about and enjoying glasses of champagne before the guests were ushered to their seats.

There was a small orchestra that were on hand to provide the music that the soprano would need and when all were ready, Aurora Ricci took her place centre stage and began to sing.

She began with a piece from La Finta Semplice, then moved into another from Dafne. Next she performed Euridice, Orfeo, and Venus and Adonis. After she sang pieces from Fidelio and La Cenerentola, she began to sing a piece that Lady Sarah had never heard before, Al dolce guidami castel natio, from one of the more recently penned operas, Anna Bolena.

As she listened to the music and was transported to the court of Henry VIII, Lady Sarah began to cry. At the end of the song, she was the first to leap to her feet and applaud.

The evening was filled with more songs, food and delightful conversation.

"Your ladyship, will you be coming to the performance of Anna Bolena in London?" Aurora asked with a genuine smile.

"Sadly, we are not. We could not get tickets," Lady

Sarah replied with a sigh.

"But I must have you there! To have someone so moved by music to miss the performance would be terrible. Please, you must all come as my guests," Aurora said as she grasped her ladyship's hands desperately.

"Then of course we will come," Lady Sarah replied.

Chapter 4

The household at Grangeback was roused from their beds by hammering on the door. Bosworth was still dressing when the knocking began in earnest, and it continued, uninterrupted, until the butler reached the door.

"What is all this noise?" the brigadier asked with annoyance as he appeared in his nightshirt and cap at the top of the main staircase.

Bosworth opened the door and on the doorstep was stood Signorina Aurora Ricci alongside a very weary looking Mr Wilbraham Egerton Senior, and Captain Jonnes Smith.

"Bosworth, our apologies for disturbing you so early this morning, but there has been some threats made against the signorina," Captain Jonnes Smith said, as he stepped through the front door.

The brigadier, upon hearing the voice of the

superintendent disappeared back to his room to dress. Mr Hunter was the first of the household to descend, fully clothed, followed by Mrs Bosworth fussing over Lady Sarah and Sylvia.

The brigadier came last, and by the time time he was ready, Sylvia was tending to the soprano as she lay collapsed on a couch in the morning room. Lady Sarah and Mr Hunter were talking to Captain Jonnes Smith and Wilbraham Egerton by the fireplace, all with very dark looks on their faces.

"What on earth has happened?" the brigadier asked with furrowed brow.

"When the signorina awoke this morning, she found a letter on her bed," Wilbraham said as he reached into his pocket and pulled out a folded piece of paper.

"What time was this?" Lady Sarah asked.

"Around 5 o'clock. The signorina has not quite become accustomed to the difference in the time between here and Naples," Wilbraham replied.

The brigadier unfolded the letter and read it through twice before passing it to his son, who read it and then passed it to Lady Sarah.

The letter read:

Go Home.

If you stay, I will kill you.

"It is to the point," Mr Hunter sighed.

"And it was on her bed? How was it delivered?" Lady Sarah frowned.

"None of the household staff remember seeing such a letter, and it was not received by the butler," the superintendent replied.

"Then someone came into Tatton Park and left the letter, which means that they could get in again and hurt the Signorina," the brigadier surmised.

"Which is why we thought it best to bring her here. At

the very least, we know that we can rely on Pattinson to defend her in this house until she travels to London. But it would also be best if she were to have a company of escorts to ensure her safety. Constable Evans has already been assigned to protect her on the journey. I understand that she has invited you all as her particular guests for her performances in London?" the captain replied.

"Yes, she was most eager to have her ladyship at her concerts," Mr Hunter said with a warm smile.

"Then could you be prevailed upon to help the constable and accompany the signorina? It is a lot to ask, but you are by no means strangers to dangerous situations and there is no one that can be trusted more. After all, the death or even murder of such a prominent soprano would do irreparable damage to our international reputation and that of our new queen," Wilbraham said in hushed tones.

"You can rely on us, sir," the brigadier said firmly.

"Good, good, I will have to return to London tonight,

but should you need any assistance, do not hesitate to reach out to me and I will do what I can," Wilbraham said with a nod.

"Constables Clewes is coming to take over Constable Evans' duty in the village whilst you travel. He will report this afternoon and then Evans will be made available to you. Until then, I would suggest that the signorina is not left alone," the captain said curtly.

"Very well, I am sure Sylvia and Mrs Bosworth will be able to keep a close watch on her until the constable arrives," the brigadier assured the two men as he accompanied them to the door to show them out.

Mr Hunter and Lady Sarah followed but paused in the doorway to the morning room where they could talk without fear of being overheard.

"What do you think?" Mr Hunter asked her in a low voice.

"That whoever is behind this letter has gone to great

lengths to deliver it and remain unseen. That speaks of a level dedication that even Lady de Mandeville would aspire to," Lady Sarah mused as her mind picked over the letter and the circumstances.

"Do you think that it should be taken so seriously?" Mr Hunter asked with a raised eyebrow.

"A death threat should always be taken seriously. At best you discover it is a poor attempt at jest. It would be far worse to ignore it and discover your folly to late to avoid disaster," Lady Sarah replied.

"Then I will fetch Pattinson from the kitchen and we will patrol the grounds," Mr Hunter said.

"I will send for the Baker boys and the doctor, I fear we shall need their assistance as well," Lady Sarah replied and kissed Mr Hunter on the cheek. "Be careful."

Chapter 5

The doctor came at once to the manor and attended the signorina. Aside from using the bathroom, there was not a single moment when the opera singer was alone whilst at the manor. Sylvia and Mrs Bosworth took it in turns to sit by her bedside and the doctor visited her three times during the day to ensure that she had recovered from the shock of it all.

When Mrs Bosworth was not looking after the singer, she was busy overseeing the packing of cases for those that would be travelling to London.

The Baker boys arrived out of breath but ready to help Mr Hunter patrol the grounds looking for any signs of interlopers.

When night fell, Constable Evans arrived at the house with Constables McIntyre, Cantello, and McGill to help guard the house whilst the inhabitants slept.

Sylvia slept in a chair by the bedside of the soprano to make sure that no one disturbed her and Pattinson guarded the window, stirring at the slightest sound.

No note was left during the night, and nothing arrived with the post the following morning. All the preparations had been made for the party to depart before lunch, and Cooky had packed quite the picnic for the party to take with them so that they would not go hungry if there was not a suitable place for them to stop before they reached their first overnight rest.

The brigadier had spent the previous day sending out telegrams to make arrangements in London and to all the best families he knew that would be able to provide the party with rooms for the night on their journey to save the group from staying at inns.

Though there were a number of fine inns that would be more than adequate on any other occasion, the brigadier thought it best to stay in secure houses with loyal staff.

Replies to the telegrams came quickly, and all were quick to offer shelter and meals to the brigadier without question.

The carriage was loaded quickly and efficiently by the coachmen and both the horses of Mr Hunter and Lady Sarah were saddled for the journey. It was thought best to bring them along, should there be a need for the singer to be extracted and the carriage abandoned.

As the final preparations were being made, two bags appeared on top of the carriage that did not look like they belonged to any member of the party. The driver questioned the source of the bags with Lady Sarah, but she simply smiled and told them to secure the baggage.

Constable Arwyn Evans, Pattinson, the brigadier, Sylvia and Aurora were to travel in the carriage. Mr Hunter and Lady Sarah would ride along side the party with two of the grooms on some of the other horses from the stable.

The doctor had no call to leave the village this time.

He was getting older and did not want to be constantly dragged on adventures around the country and beyond. A walking holiday with the reverend was more than enough excitement for him.

Signorina Ricci had recovered from her shock at receiving the death threat and was in no medical danger, so Doctor Jack Hales could return to his home and practice, and sit by his fire and enjoy the comforts of home.

As the carriage lurched forward the signorina gave a cry of surprise as two faces appeared from above. The faces of Lee and Stanley Baker peered down into the carriage from the roof.

The brigadier burst into laughter at the site of the two boys and with great care, helped the two of them climb down from the roof into the carriage.

"What is the meaning of this?" Aurora demanded crossly. "There has been a threat on my life and these two urchins appear from nowhere, and you help them into the carriage!"

"Calm yourself," the brigadier said sternly. "These boys are far from being mere urchins. They are two of the most promising detectives that England has ever known. To have them with us is a blessing. With them helping her ladyship, the constable, Sylvia, and my son, you can be certain that your would-be murderer will be caught before any harm can befall you."

Pattinson raised his head and briefly licked the legs of the boys before settling down again at their feet.

"It is now too cramped. Someone will have to get out," the signer snapped and looked at the unimpressed faces of her companions.

"If you wish to walk, no one will stop you," Sylvia said dryly and turned her head to look out the window.

The carriage was the largest one in the brigadier's possession and it comfortably sat eight fully grown men. It was a large coach that had been terribly expensive, but it was the most luxurious vehicle in the neighbourhood. The brigadier had two smaller carriages and a break, but none of them were suitable for a trip as far as London.

Arwyn stifled a chuckle at the dry sarcasm the lady's maid displayed and the pair earned dark looks from both the soprano.

Though she scowled, she did not say another word as the carriage lumbered on. Outside, Lady Sarah and Mr Hunter rode beside one another behind the carriage and revelled in the peace and quiet of the road, compared to the noise coming from the interior of the carriage.

Chapter 6

The signorina made several more complaints

during the journey, but all of them were ignored. Her protests

at the room she was given at each of the homes they visited

on the journey down fell on deaf ears. Constable Evans took

her to her room and secured it, and Sylvia sat beside her bed

throughout the night to ensure that she was safe.

Parties were organised to patrol the grounds during

the night. During the day the party travelled in the carriage.

Lee and Stanley Baker slept as they were part of the ground

patrols.

The soprano complained about the noise of the two

boys snoring but harsh looks from the brigadier and Sylvia

was soon silenced.

By the time the group reached Covent Garden, the

opera singer had burned through any goodwill that had

existed amongst the party accompanying her.

The brigadier did not disembark with the others, but took the carriage and all of the horses to the Ritz Hotel with their baggage to ensure that their rooms would be ready for them.

The caretaker of the theatre opened the door to allow the party entry into the theatre where they found quite the ensemble gathered around the stage.

"Oh, Signorina Ricci! You are finally here. It is such a pleasure to see you here at our little concert hall," a tall and thin man with a French accent said grandly as he noticed the soprano.

At being recognised the signorina stepped forward and away from those protecting her. She strode forward with melodramatic grief and collapsed into the arms of the man.

"Monsieur Lavingne! It has been a most terrible journey. And the threats!" Aurora sobbed.

"Threats? Threats? What threats? And who are these

people with you?" the Frenchman asked with a furrowed brow.

"My name is Lady Sarah Montgomery Baird Watson-Wentworth, with me are Mr Alexander Hunter Webb-Kneelingroach, heir to the Grangeback Estate in Cheshire, my companion, Sylvia Edwards, the signorina's bodyguard, Constable Arwyn Evans, and my sometimes wards, Lee and Stanley Baker," Lady Sarah said. "And this fine canine is Pattinson. Who might you be?"

"Ah, your ladyship, my deepest apologies for my rudeness. I am Monsieur Jacques Lavingne, the manager of this theatre. Perhaps you could enlighten me as to the threats the signorina mentioned, and then I shall introduce you to the rest of our little chorus," the theatre manager said as he moved the opera singer to the stalls so she could sit whilst he listened to what Lady Sarah and her friends had to say.

"After performing at a salon at Tatton Park, the signorina received a death threat. The chief constable assigned Constable Evans as her bodyguard and requested that we travel down with the signorina to protect her," Lady Sarah said calmly.

"I see, then it is understandable that she would be in such a state. Come Signorina Aurora, you can rest in your dressing room," Jacques said and waved in the direction of backstage.

"I will take her, I think it is best if she is not left alone," Sylvia offered her hand to the soprano and with a glance at Lady Sarah, walked the singer to her dressing room.

"Let us introduce you to our little ensemble," Jacques said and led the group to the stage where a young brunette beauty was laughing at the joke of an ageing lothario, a small man with a balding head wringing his fingers, a stiff-backed man with a hook nose and a shock of untamed hair, and a quiet-looking man with tanned skin.

"This beautiful young woman is Miss Jenny Lind, the signorina's understudy. She has been a devotee of the craft and though she is young, she is a great talent. This tall rascal

is Hector Jamieson, an fine actor with no signing ability but

when asked to perform Shakespeare, there is none finer,"

Jacques said as he approached the stage.

"Ah, another beautiful lady graces us with her

presence," Hector said grandly and bowed low.

"Oh stop your fussing," the balding man said crossly.

"And this fine man is our stage manager, Mr Ernest

Boult. A man of great precision and timing that we could not

live without,"

"Please, Monsieur, there are only a few hours left in

the day, we must being rehearsing now the signorina has

finally arrived," the hook-nosed man said with irritation.

"And this is our esteemed conductor, Herr Bruno

Wagner," Jacques said with a smile.

"No relation," the conductor said quickly and with a

measure of distaste.

"You are not enamoured by the work of Herr Richard

Wagner?" Lady Sarah asked with bemusement.

"I have been a conductor far longer than he has been composing and yet now it is the first question I am asked," Herr Wagner replied.

"I understand your frustration," Mr Hunter said with a slight nod that seemed to smooth some of the conductors ruffled feathers.

"And finally, this young man with the violin is Señor Julio Mendez, our lead violinist," the theatre manager finished the introductions and Lady Sarah proceeded to introduce her party, but as she was speaking, a great scream shook the theatre.

Mr Hunter, the constable, and the Baker boys all set off running towards the source of the scream at a run, followed by Ernest Boult.

"Ladies, do not fear, I will protect you!" Hector announced bravely. Pattinson barked his disapproval and caused the actor to jump in alarm.

"Perhaps we should sit and wait for the others in the stalls," Lady Sarah suggested and Jacques agreed that it was a good idea, as he glanced nervously towards the backstage area.

As the group sat down and waited for news, Pattinson walked up and down the row of people and sniffed each in turn, clearly making some form of judgement about the individuals.

Sylvia appeared a short time later, looking quite pale and came to kneel beside Lady Sarah.

"I think you should go to the dressing room. I will stay here with Pattinson and the others," Sylvia said with a trembling voice.

"Are you all right?" Lady Sarah asked with concern.

"I am. You will see the cause of the scream, but there is something else. I saw something, a figure, a menacing figure reflected in the mirror, but when I turned to face it, it had vanished," Sylvia explained.

"Stay here, Pattinson will ensure no harm comes to you. No spirit, spectre or monster can hurt you with him beside you," Lady Sarah said warmly.

"Please, be careful," Sylvia implored her employer as she took her seat. Lady Sarah smiled reassuringly and patted the drawstring purse on her arm.

"I will be."

Her ladyship made her way to the back of the theatre, reaching into her bag and drawing out her pearl handled revolver as soon as she was out of sight of the theatre ensemble.

The report from Sylvia of the figure in the mirror had set the lady's nerves on edge and she was cautious as she made her way to the dressing room. Though every creak and cough made her mind spin, there was nothing out of place in the stillness of the theatre.

Mr Hunter was waiting for her outside the signorina's dressing room.

"She fainted. I am surprised that Sylvia did not faint as well given what she saw," he announced as he saw his fiancée approaching.

"It has certainly jangled her nerves somewhat. But she is with Pattinson and is sat with the others, she will recover. Will the signorina?" Lady Sarah asked as she put her revolver away.

"Who can say? Mr Boult has put her on her couch for now to rest and sent one of his boys to fetch a doctor. When father arrives, I think he should fetch the police. Arwyn is looking over everything now but he has no official power outside of Cheshire," Alex said with a shrug.

"Where are Lee and Stanley?" her ladyship frowned as she looked around for any sign of the two boys.

"They have gone in search of the figure. I don't know what they will find, but they have faithfully promised not to die and to yell if they get into trouble," Mr Hunter said with a shake of his head.

"Do not tell their mother," Lady Sarah sighed and followed Mr Hunter into the dressing room.

The room was nothing special, save for the decorative folding partition that had a large fainting couch poking out from behind it upon which the feet of the signorina could be seen.

There was a large dressing table that was covered with make-up and ornate wigs on stands and had a giant, ornate mirror mounted upon the wall behind it facing the door. A matching full-length mirror stood at the opposite end of the room to the partition and there was a rail filled with costumes beside it.

Upon the mirror mounted on the wall, a message was written.

You were warned.

Go Home or Die.

Now, you will not leave

this theatre alive.

It was written in some form of red mixture that was thick enough to paint the words with but thin enough to drip down the mirror.

"I thought it might be blood at first, but up close it does not look the same," Arwyn explained as he watched the young lady examining the mirror.

"No, it is a mixture of water and rouge that is used as a form of make-up for the stage. I suspect that it is from one of these make-up palettes, I find it unlikely that whoever did this brought make-up with them," Lady Sarah said as she looked at the palettes until she found the right one.

"How does that help you find out who did this?" Mr Boult asked crossly from behind the screen.

"It tells us that whoever did this is not a stranger. They know this theatre and they are most likely to still be here," Lady Sarah replied as she tapped the palette on the edge of the dressing table.

"What do we do now? You know I am only supposed to stay until the morning and then ride back on Harald," the constable said.

"We stay and protect the signorina and try to find out who is behind these threats before they can carry them out," Lady Sarah shrugged.

"What about Captain Jonnes Smith?" Arwyn asked.

"I am sure that Mr Egerton will convince him of the need for your presence here, but we can only stay if the theatre manager allows it, so we must speak with him before we do anything else," her ladyship said firmly.

Chapter 7

The doctor arrived quickly and insisted that the signorina be moved from her dressing room into a different one, away from the mirror that Constable Evans refused to allow the theatre staff to clean.

Lee and Stanley Baker returned not long after the doctor arrived with the news that they had managed to find nothing during their search.

Sylvia's colour had returned to her cheeks and she looked much more like her normal self when the detective party rejoined the group. The brigadier had arrived in the interim and Sylvia had told him everything.

He waited long enough to see with his own eyes that his son and ward were both safe before he went to fetch the police.

Jacques was beside himself with worry and looked as

though he would be violently ill at any moment.

"Please, constable, Miss Edwards tells me that you are going to leave us, but you must stay. You must protect the signorina!" the theatre manager begged Arwyn, who reluctantly agreed and went to stand guard over the singer whilst the doctor tended to her.

Sylvia agreed to go with him and took Pattinson to help, leaving Lady Sarah, Mr Hunter and the Baker boys to investigate.

Lady Sarah knew that though Sylvia looked as though she was fully recovered, there was something about the theatre that scared her and that the safest place would be where Arwyn and Pattinson were.

Mr Hunter and the young lady had both been in more than their fair share of dangerous situations since Sylvia had known them both, and experience told her that if she investigated this mystery with them, she would find herself face-to-face with the menacing figure once more.

For Lee and Stanley Baker, the danger and seeing the menacing figure for themselves was the draw of investigating this mystery.

Lady Sarah did not relish the task of protecting the young boys whilst she investigated the mystery, but she knew they would be an asset in a place where smaller bodies could reach areas that she and Mr Hunter could not.

The theatre manager herded the remaining members of the ensemble to the foyer where comfortable sofas and seats had been laid out by Mr Boult, as well as a course of refreshments to keep them all comfortable whilst they were waiting for the police to arrive.

Lady Sarah did not think it was necessary to have the group be watched over whilst they began to search the backstage area.

Lee and Stanley had been searching for a figure but little else on, and though they had the palette that had been used to create the writing there was no sign of the brush that had been used. None of the brushes on the signorina's

dressing table were wet or dyed with the same red as the

concoction on the mirror.

When they had first looked at the dressing room

nothing struck the party as being out of place. Even now as

they returned to the scene, not a thing appeared to be wrong -

save for the threat written on the mirror. Everything seemed

to belong in such a world as far as they could tell.

Nothing had been knocked over or disturbed, and

nothing could seemingly be moved. The screen was bolted to

the floor, the mirror bolted to the wall and the full length

mirror was too heavy to move without two people lifting it.

"Perhaps we should begin by discussing how they

might kill this signorina," Mr Hunter suggested as he felt a bit

of a loss as what they should be focusing on.

"Sadly we have an almost infinite number of ways

that she may come to harm within a place such as this. Until

we know more about whomever it is that is leaving these

messages, we can only speculate on how they might go about

carrying out their threat," Lady Sarah replied with a sigh.

"Then we search the room?" Mr Hunter asked with a

weary shake of his head.

"Yes, and search for that bag of grain," Lady Sarah

said with a slight smile. When the pair had first met, Mr

Hunter was accused of a crime he didn't commit and the bag

of grain in his home had been one of many clues Lady Sarah

had found that proved his innocence.

After 15 minutes of fruitless searching, they concluded

there was nothing else to be found in the dressing room.

"What now?" Lee asked as he slumped against the

wall with a disappointed look on his face.

"Now the pair of you must go looking for the brush

elsewhere. This theatre is filled with all sorts of hiding places,

all manner of nooks, crannies, bins, anything that you can

think of that might have been used to hide a make-up brush

in," Lady Sarah said explicitly and the two boys set off to

carry out their task like a shot.

"Are you sure a brush was used?" Mr Hunter frowned.

"There are definite strokes within the powder mix," Lady Sarah said. "You don't get those lines without using a brush."

Mr Hunter was less than convinced, so Lady Sarah reached into her purse and pulled out the palette. Pulling off one of her white lace gloves, she pick up one of the make-up brushes from the dressing table as well as a small piece of sponge.

She used her finger first to draw on the full-length mirror, then on used the sponge and finally used the brush.

"Can you now see the difference between the three? The effect they make is quite stark in contrast," Lady Sarah asked as she admired her own handiwork.

"Yes, when using the sponge, it barely leaves any impression on the glass at all. With your finger, it's very uneven and the brush is much harder to tell, though looks more like handwriting," the hunter observed.

Lady Sarah looked to him quizzically looked at the mirror that she had written on and looked back at the mirror bolted to the wall.

"That is not something I had considered," she said as she rubbed her rouge coloured finger across her bottom lip. Mr Hunter smiled to himself at he sight of the stained lip of the young lady but Lady Sarah was oblivious as she was focused on the handwriting.

"I wonder what this could tell us. In fact it might be easier to find this suspect than I imagined," she said slowly. "Stay here and guard the mirror. Perhaps clean off our mirror so that when the police arrive they do not think more messages have been left," she said to Mr Hunter and without any further mention she darted back to the foyer.

"Oh Lady Sarah, have you found anything? what happened to your lip? Oh, so many questions that I have for you. I don't know where to begin!" Jacques babbled as Lady Sarah appeared in the lobby. Lady Sarah reached out and calmed him with a simple touch from her hand upon his arm.

"Monsieur, would you be so kind as to fetch some paper and pencils?" she asked in a low voice.

"But of course! Why my lady? may I ask?" the theatre manager enquired.

"I simply want to see the styles in which everyone in the theatre writes or if they can write at all," Lady Sarah replied with a slight smile.

"I understand," Jacques said with a nod of his head and he disappeared off into the ticket office to find some paper and pencils. He returned presently and gave out a pencil and paper to each of those assembled.

"What would you like us to write, my lady?" Hector asked, as he burnished his pencil as though it were an extension of himself.

"I would like you to write the following: my name is

Zelda. I own a xylophone. Rum cake is for the queen. That should be quiet enough," Lady Sarah smiled and watched each of the ensemble attempting to write.

Julio, however, put down the pencil and paper and very meekly walked over to her ladyship.

"I am afraid I cannot write nor can I read. I can only read music," he said in a small voice.

"That is quite all right. Thank you," Lady Sarah said with a slight smile.

"You are most gracious, my Lady. May I go and practice?" the violinist asked with a hopeful look in his eye.

"Yes, I am sure that you will come to no harm practising in the dress circle, but please do not stray from there. I am sure the police will have as many questions for you, as they will do for all of us," Lady Sarah says said kindly. "Perhaps Herr Wagner, you might wish to accompany him?" Lady Sarah asked as she looked at the conductor who had finished writing.

"That is an excellent idea, my lady," Bruno said as he stood up, straightened his coat, and led the way to the dress circle.

The theatre manager collected Wagner's piece of paper with his own and presented them to Lady Sarah.

It did not take long for Hector and Jenny to finish writing either.

"What of Mr Boult? Can he read and write?" Lady Sarah asked

"I believe he cannot but there is no harm in taking a pencil and paper to him and quietly inquiring whether he will write out the same sentences," Jacques said.

"Excellent, thank you so much," Lady Sarah said as she sat down on one of the sofas.

The theatre manage set off with a pen and pencil in hand to find where the stage manager had disappeared to.

He had been in the dressing room with the doctor, keen to oversee the treatment of the signorina. However, upon his arrival at the dressing room, Sylvia informed the theatre manager that the stage manager had disappeared some time ago.

Whilst Jacques attempted to discover the whereabouts of Mr Boult, Lady Sarah was sat in a most uncomfortable silence with Hector and Jenny.

"If you'll excuse me, Lady Sarah, I am in need of answering nature's call," Hector announced suddenly as he stood up and with slight now, disappeared into the theatre, leaving Jenny alone with Lady Sarah.

"Can I asked what exactly it is that you're looking for? Asking for us to write out those very strange lines?" the understudy asked.

"It is quite simple. A brush was used to write that message upon the mirror. When using a brush it is not that dissimilar to using a pencil. There is a style to the writing. It is not identical, because you hold the brush at a different point than you would a pencil. However, it does help us to see who might have left the message and who is worth investigating," Lady Sarah said.

"So Julio and Mr Boult, because they cannot write, would not have left the message?" Jenny asked as she followed lead Sarah's line of thinking.

"Whoever left the message had to be able to read and write which narrows pools of suspects, would you not say?" the young lady said with a blank expression on her face.

"But then you suspect me?" Jenny asked coyly.

"Of course. An understudy has a lot to gain from her Prima Dona not performing," Lady Sarah replied with a smile, which didn't quite reach her eyes.

"And you do not want any one of us to be alone for too long. Which is why you sent the conductor and violinist to rehearse together," Jenny said logically.

"No, indeed," Lady Sarah agreed. The two sat for quite some time chatting and smiling about nothing in particular.

Music was their chief shared interest, but it barely came up between the exchange of pleasantries. Lady Sarah found herself liking the opera singer. However, liking and being able to trust her were two very different things.

It was some time before Hector returned from his trip to the bathroom and when he did, he seemed quite cross.

"Is everything all right?" Lady Sarah asked.

"Quite fine. Thank you," Hector snapped at her and then remembered himself. "My dear ladies, it is nothing to fret yourselves over. Everything will be well. Those two boys you have running around in the backstage area. A slight inconvenience that is all."

Lady Sarah didn't quite believe him, but chose not to press the matter.

The theatre manager took even longer to return with Mr. Bolt, and another blank piece of paper. Lady Sarah required no explanation and merely nodded her thanks to the theatre and stage managers.

When the group was reassembled in the foyer, save for the violinist and conductor, Lady Sarah waited patiently for the suspects to write on their pieces of paper, and then returned to Mr Hunter with the copies of handwriting.

"What did you discover?" Mr Hunter asked, with a slightly bored tone in his voice.

"I discovered a great many things. I discovered that Jenny is extremely clever, and far more so than she would have you believe. I discovered that Hector is hiding a great many things to the extent that he changed his handwriting from one sentence to another. It took a great length of time for Monsignor Levine to locate Mr Bolt and come back with blank pieces of paper - far longer than it should in fact. I suspected that the violinist could not write. In fact, I'm surprised that so many of our assembled ensemble with European backgrounds can write and speak English so well. The señor seems to have a basic command of English, enough to get by you whilst touring great opera houses, but I suspect that he would find it with a great struggle to write even the most basic message," Lady Sarah replied.

"So he is not a suspect?" Mr Hunter asked with a slight glimmer of amusement on his face.

"For the moment, he is at the bottom of our list," Lady Sarah smiled.

"What of the others?" Mr Hunter sighed as he looked over the pages.

"I think that Hector has jumped leaps and bounds with, Mr Boult, to the top of that list. But for now, I think we should lock this room and return to them in the lobby and await the police," Lady Sarah replied. For the briefest moment she had the glimmer of an epiphany but it was gone almost instantly.

"Yes, I think you're right," Mr. Hunter said.

A moment or two later, scrambling and cheering could be heard in the corridors as Lee and Stanley Baker returned, brandishing the brush in their hand.

"I see you found it," Lady Sarah said with a smile. But it was not a make-up brush they were holding, but a paintbrush. It was the kind that an artist might use on a canvas.

"Now that is interesting," she said. "I wonder who in this company might paint."

"I believe Mr Boult has just become your prime suspect," Mr Hunter said with a slight smile.

"Perhaps he has," Lady Sarah allowed. "Where did you find the brush?" she asked with apparent curiosity.

"That was hidden under a collapsed bit of scenery. We wouldn't have found it if we hadn't been trying to get out of the way of that stupid actor. He was trying to push his way down the backstage. Don't know where he was going," Lee Baker explained.

"The backstage behind the stage," Lady Sarah frowned.

"Yes," Stanley said. "He seemed to be in a big hurry to

get somewhere. And in an even greater hurry to get back.
Even pushed me over. That's when we found it. The
paintbrush."

"And what have you been doing since then?" Lady
Sarah asked with a raised eyebrow.

"Well, we'll have to show you," Stanley said with a
grin.

"What a good job you both snuck aboard the
carriage," Lady Sarah said with relief.

Chapter 8

The brigadier returned to the theatre with two reluctant constables in tow. The pair were less than enthused about the situation and even less willing to investigate the scene.

The hysteria of Jacques and Hector did not help the situation either, the pair becoming more and more melodramatic with each fact they related.

The two constables listened with bemused looks on their faces for a short time before declaring that it was probably just kids playing a mean spirited practical joke on the theatre.

Lady Sarah, Mr Hunter and Constable Evans were nowhere to be seen when the police arrived and they were unwilling to wait for the trio to be found. The two constables left without bothering to write anything in their pocket notebooks.

The brigadier was less than enthused by their lack of interest in the mystery, and turned on his heel to go speak with the chief constable to impress upon him the seriousness of the situation at Covent Garden.

Meanwhile, Lady Sarah and Mr Hunter were being led through the maze of stored scenery at the back of the stage whilst the police were supposedly listening to the theatre manager and actor in the foyer.

Lee and Stanley Baker had made an extensive search of the area and turned up far more than the artist's paintbrush.

At the back of the scenery store there was a small shelter that contained some morsels of food that had not been found by the rats, a handful of blankets, and a straw bed. Bundled up as a pillow for that bed were a thick black cape, black trousers and a black shirt.

"Curious," Lady Sarah said with a wry smile as she

looked at the contents of the shelter. "You both did excellent work, truly excellent," Lady Sarah beamed at the two boys.

"I will fetch Sylvia, and ask her if these could be the clothes she saw the figure in," Mr Hunter said, and disappeared back through the maze.

"We will wait here and guard it in case they come back," Lee said firmly and Stanley nodded in agreement. Lady Sarah leaned down and kissed both boys on the top of their heads in a motherly fashion.

"Please, be careful. If they return and do not run, you must. I do not want the pair of you injured over a pile of clothing," Lady Sarah told the boys with a firm voice.

"We promise," Stanley said with a grin.

Lady Sarah knew there was nothing else she could do in the scenery maze for the moment, and that any adult would struggle to follow where the two Baker boys could squeeze through, should they need to run.

The most pressing matter was to now talk to each of

the ensemble in turn about their part in the signorina's life, and to find out what, if anything, she could learn about who might have a motive to want her dead.

None of the stage hands had arrived to work that day as during these first few rehearsals they were not needed. Only the stage manager, and the conductor had to be in attendance, which made Lady Sarah wonder why the rest of the troupe were there.

Her ladyship decided the best way to interview each of the suspects was to surreptitiously separate them. She began with Monsieur Jack Levine, out of all the suspects, he was the one that stood to lose the most should anything happen to the signorina. People paid to come to the opera to see the leading ladies, not just for music that was played.

Therefore, if anything were to happen to her, the theatre manager would be the one to suffer. In order to speak to him without arousing suspicion, Lady Sarah took him to one side to under the guise of preparing the stage for rehearsals to ensure everything was safe.

When she was sure no one else was listening, she began her questioning of the monsieur.

"What can you tell me about the signorina? Has she ever performed here before?" Lady Sarah asked nonchalantly as the two walked down to the stage.

"She has not performed here before, but I have had the honour of working with her in France, and again in Italy in my younger years, I'd always hoped to bring her here to perform. She is an excellent singer. Though, her personality leaves something to be desired," Jacques said with a slight smile.

Lady Sarah nodded knowingly.

"Yes, she does have a way of insisting on certain things," she said with a slight giggle.

"Indeed. But as a diva and prima donna, I suppose that is her prerogative," the theatre manager shrugged.

"Yeah. I can understand the temperament of such a

singer could be very volatile. Has anything like this ever happened before that you know of?" Lady Sarah enquired.

"No. But there was said to be some business with her sister. Many many years ago. I heard she died in some form of accident. You've heard of sister, of course," the monsieur said in an offhand manner. Lady Sarah shook her head.

"They were twins. I believe both aspiring opera singers. However, something happened to the twin. She drank something that damaged her throat. Someone supposedly put acid in a beaker to stop her from singing. Whether it was the signorina herself or someone else was never quite established. But by all reports her sister died as a result of drinking the concoction," Jacques said.

"That it's very interesting indeed," Lady Sarah said as the pair walked around the stage comparing notes about the relative safety and any issues that might arise from people being on the stage. As well as any potential murder weapons, including falling scenery, a gun from the wings, and a knife throwing act that may have snuck in unbeknownst to anyone else. They clearly ranged from the practical to the ridiculous, but Lady Sarah was willing to entertain any idea at this point as to how harm might come to the signorina.

After questioning the theatre manager, Mr Hunter joined her in the foyer. He took her to one side and quietly whispered,

"Silvia can't be sure, but she thinks they might be the same clothes the beggar was wearing. All black is a little bit nondescript," Mr Hunter said. "But surely it would not be that unusual for a stage hand to wear black."

"I do not think that they take such things into consideration. I have to confess I never paid much attention to the stage hands before any performance," Lady Sarah replied with a slight frown.

"Yes, one doesn't pay attention to the help," Mr Hunter said quite pointedly, with his eyebrow raised.

"Come now, you know that's not what I meant," Lady

Sarah said apologetically. "But you are right. Stage hands can move about without being seen by most, mainly because they're not supposed to be seen. All attention is supposed to focus on the performance."

"Have you questioned all of the stage hands yet?" Mr Hunter asked, changing the subject, knowing that further discussion could only lead to an argument between the pair.

"Not yet. I've only spoken to the theatre manager so far. I was going to talk to Miss Lind next. Would you perhaps be willing to talk to Mr Boult? You might be better at talking to him than I," Lady Sarah said with a wry smile.

"Working man to working man you mean?" Mr Hunter asked with good humour.

"Perhaps," Lady Sarah replied with a shrug.

"I will do my best to find out what I can from him," Mr Hunter agreed, and with a brief kiss on his lady's hand, the pair went their separate ways to continue their questioning.

Miss Lind knew almost nothing. She was quite candid about the motivation she may have for removing the signorina from the picture. Especially given that she would be the one singing instead of the soprano, should anything terrible happen.

However, she did allow that many people would be disappointed and ask for refunds on our tickets should she be the one to perform in the prima donna's place.

Lady Sarah was more than satisfied that Miss Lind was not involved. In fact, for all her candour, she was sure that this woman was actually a very pretty and sweet young lady who would do very well for herself should she be given the opportunity she needed to advance.

After Miss Lind, Lady Sarah spoke to Hector Jamieson. For all his bravado, he was very bad at hiding the fact that he was intentionally trying to divert Lady Sarah's attention away from certain questions.

"My dear sir, if you do not stop with all of your tricks

and sleight of hand, your word games etc. we shall never be finished talking," Lady Sarah said quite pointedly.

"Direct and to the point," Hector allowed. "What is it you wish to know?" he said, his voice changing from the grandiose speech that he would normally use to a much more common turn of phrase. The tone of his voice changed as well. So much so, Lady Sarah could hear cockney origins lurking beneath his practised tone.

"You were not born to wealthy," Lady Sarah observed, with a raised eyebrow.

"Not in the slightest," he replied. "I was lucky. My parents didn't have much in the way of money but we were never made to go hungry. And the moment they could, they apprenticed me to the theatre. I was always a bit too - flamboyant - to go into something such as chimney sweeping or being a merchant of some sort. I was given an education in the theatre. I started as a stage hand, watching the craft from the back, and eventually was allowed small walk on parts.

Until I became who you see today. A man of great talent, of great poise, and most importantly, a man who has had a great career," he said with a without embellishment.

"Indeed. So why the pretence, why the persona that you adopt around other people?" Lady Sarah frowned.

"It is always a game of pretence in the theatre. You never quite know who to trust," Hector said candidly.

"If you are a man to place money on who to trust in this great game is there anyone that you could?" Lady Sarah asked, looking at the actor with a new found respect.

"Aside from yourself, my lady? No. Everyone else has too much to gain, and too much to lose by being honest," Hector replied.

"And what do you have to lose?" Lady Sarah pressed the actor.

"Me? Nothing. I lost much long ago. You see, I was once engaged to the signorina. It was a love affair for the ages. I met her whilst I was touring with a company of players. We were desperately in love. It was a passionate affair. So much so we were set to be married not long after meeting, but alas, it was not to be. She had an opportunity to perform, to become greater than I was. She departed before the wedding so I was left with nothing. Her career blossom blossomed, and mine dimmed. I play the older roles now. Falstaff and such. But I bear her no ill will. My career did not suffer for the lack of her in it. My life perhaps, but we shall never know now," Hector sighed deeply.

"Very well. Thank you. I appreciate you being so open with me," Lady Sarah smiled sadly at the man who had pain etched on his face. It was a pain she had felt all too recently and though her love had been restored to her, and all was forgiven, she could imagine how deeply the pain would sit in the heart.

"And who is it that you would like to see next for your interrogations?" Hector asked with a grin.

"I think perhaps Señor Mendez should answer the

next few questions," Lady Sarah said.

"Very good. I will tell him you wish to hear his violin solo that he has to play on opening night.

With a bow to the lady, Hector left her to sit and promised he would not tell the assembled company about the questioning. After all, to be in the theatre was to pretend.

Hector had been more than emphatic on that point. However to say that and then announced such a motive to her, Lady Sarah considered that it could be a double bluff.

But in announcing that he had no ill will, to tell her so freely of their past together. That she would just count him out as a suspect.

She mused on the thought until Señor Mendez arrived, his violin in hand. She listened politely until he finished playing and after she gave him sufficient applause for the musical treat that he had provided, Lady Sarah sat him down began speaking to him surprisingly, in his native tongue.

"Why is it that you are here now? Surely only the conductor, prima donna, and theatre manager are required so early before the performance," Lady Sarah said.

The violinist was taken aback for a moment upon hearing his language, but recovered himself quickly enough.

"It's been a long time since you have been to the theatre or even an opera house. In a performance, there are many moving parts. Although it used to be custom that only a few were called at a time. It is now imperative that we have so many of us together so that we may perform cohesively. The Signora will sing over my violin, increasing her pitch to overpower my notes, it is something I must know. There are times I will have to play more quietly. Equally there are moments where, if the signorina cannot reach a certain note, I may have to play louder to cover for her shortfall. I cannot discover this without being here at rehearsals without her voice," Julio explained with fervour.

"I see. This is something I had never thought about

before. But you have played in a great number of impressive venues. You must have performed with the signorina before?" Lady Sarah asked with interest.

"I have not played with her before, but I have seen her perform. She was much younger then, her voice has matured with her, but as a voice matures, it becomes harder for certain notes to be hit. The voice wears out much like the strings of a violin," Señor Mendez explained.

"Well a violin string can be replaced, but a voice, however, that is a little harder to replace," Lady Sarah with a slight smile.

"I'm sure in this, the signorina would agree," Julio said wryly.

"I can understand then why you, and Miss Lind, would both be here, she must know the ins and outs of the performance if she has to cover for a sick signorina or if the signorina should not be able to perform for any reason. But what of the actor? Surely there's no need for him to be here,"

Lady Sarah said with a frown.

"This particular opera has had a role added to it specifically for Hector. He is finishing his career. It is his last hurrah, as you might say, his swan song. So he has a non-singing walk-on part to say farewell to the audiences of London. We are going to tour the rest of Europe and say goodbye on his behalf to the other stages. He has a great talent that will be sadly missed," the violinist said with clear regret in his voice.

"Why is it he is retiring?" Lady Sarah asked with a frown.

"No one quite knows for sure. He has not said anything nor confirmed or denied any rumours," Julio said with shrug.

"How can you be sure this is his last hurrah as you say?" Lady Sarah pressed the musician.

"It is simple really. I heard him arguing with Monsieur Lavingne about his future," Julio replied.

"But why now?" Lady Sarah wondered aloud.

"It has something to do with the signorina; some form of secret. I heard nothing more than that," Señor Mendez said a little more firmly than was necessary.

"I see. So you feel that Hector has more than a good enough motive for wanting to harm her?" Lady Sarah asked.

"Possibly, but no more than anyone else here, myself included," the musician offered.

"And why would you have a vendetta against her?" Lady Sarah frowned.

"Me? Well, that is easy. She did not want me to perform with her. She was adamant that some other violinist would be chosen. A second rate fiddler that she has apparently had a tumultuous affair with on many occasions especially during the time she was supposedly in a relationship with Mr Jamieson," Julio replied flatly.

"Then he has an even greater motive for wanting to harm her," Lady Sarah said to herself.

"Indeed, but Monsieur Lavingne stood firm and it made sure that I was hired. I believe it was Herr Bruno who wanted me here more than anyone else," Julio finished his explanation.

"I see. Thank you," Lady Sarah said as she started to speak in English again.

"Do you wish to speak to Herr Wagner now?" Julio asked, following her lead.

"Yes, I do," Lady Sarah said with the warmest smile she could muster.

"I shall ask him to come to you," the violinist said as he bowed to her and left briskly.

She sat and thought more about all that she had learned so far. Herr Bruno Wagner took his time in coming to meet with Lady Sarah.

The conductor was affronted at being questioned in such a manner and was determined to make his displeasure known.

"I must protest," he announced when he finally appeared. "I am not a criminal nor should I be treated as such. You have made your assessment, I do not doubt,   and I suspect you know of a great many motivations that there are for wishing harm on such a diva," he said brusquely.

"Perhaps the signorina is a devotee of the other Wagner," Lady Sarah said dryly and received a withering look from the conductor.

"A true noble knows that it is not nice to make fun of people," the conductor said with his nose in the air.

"A true gentleman does not question a lady's heritage or upbringing. Perhaps you should try not to be offended by being asked to answer simple questions to prove your innocence," Lady Sarah replied with a sharp tongue.

Bruno looked at her and studied her face for a few moments.

"I see, and what is it you have asked the others?" Herr Wagner asked, his icy demeanour softening slightly.

"Nothing complex. Just questions about their motivations for wanting to harm the signorina, the motivations they believe that others hold for harming her. That is it," Lady Sarah confirmed.

"I see. And you expect me to incriminate myself?" the conductor scoffed.

"On the contrary, I expect you to incriminate others, and try to deflect suspicion from yourself," Lady Sarah said flatly.

"Then I'm delighted to disappoint you my lady. As for my motivations, simply the signorina is a horrid woman who has destroyed many careers of many friends, and if I could, I would destroy her career without a single second of regret," Herr Bruno said with no small amount of spite.

"Are there any friends in particular that you can think of that might wish her harm. What of her sister, the others have said that you knew her," Lady Sarah had decided that as the conductor was being hostile towards her, she would not employ the same tact that she had with the others.

"I did indeed. Some might say intimately," Bruno replied,

"Intimately?" Lady Sarah frowned.

"Well, as intimately as a fiancé might know his fiancée," he replied with a shrug.

"You were engaged to the signorina's sister?" Lady Sarah's eyes were wide with shock.

"Yes. When she died, I was heartbroken. I walked away from music for many years. I did not want to be around it without her to sing beside me. We had a partnership you see. A long and loving partnership one that I have never held with another. I have not even wanted to try to," Herr Bruno shook his head.

"Do you blame the signorina for the death of her sister?" Lady Sarah asked.

"I do not blame her for anything. I know she is the cause of it. I hold her responsible for her death.   Blame is too passive and emotion for what I feel. And I would not only readily ruin her career, I would gladly kill her. But I would not be so foolish as to announce it. I would do something similar to what she did to her sister. I would make it so that she would suffer and she would know before the end, that I was the reason that she was suffering and why," Herr Wagner said with venom. "And what are the motivations of this queer ensemble? I suspect that Mr Boult has a far higher desire for vengeance upon the signorina then anyone else here, but that something based purely on rumour. I am sure your Mr Hunter is speaking with him."

"You do study people rather well," Lady Sarah allowed.

"In my business, you have to study people, to understand them to work out when they are lying. It is what makes the theatre the theatre of course, pretence, but to know when one is acting, and one is flat out lying is how one survives," the conductor shrugged. "Is there anything else I might help you with?"

"No, thank you," Lady Sarah said. The conductor nodded and left without another word.

It took some time for Mr Hunter to stop Mr Boult from scurrying about the theatre in order to talk with him. The stage manager was reluctant to be alone with a towering hunter.

It was something that the Hunter had gotten used to over many years. He'd always been tall and strong for his age. Working outside on his father's estate as a boy had made him an imposing figure. He was rather soft at times. He did not like doing harm to others but would defend himself and his friends should her have to.

Of course, this was something that Mr Boult didn't know. It wasn't until Mr Hunter cornered him in the backstage area that he finally managed to get some answers.

"Please, sir, I have nothing to offer you, nothing I can give you just leave me alone," Mr Boult begged.

"Sir, I'm not here to do you any harm. I merely want to ask you a few questions on behalf of her ladyship," Mr Hunter said. "They are really questions about what about the signorina, about why you fuss over her as none of the others seem to be as concerned as you are for her welfare. What has she ever done to endear herself to you."

"Nothing," the stage manager said with a shrug. "In fact, she has done everything possible to ensure that I am alienated from her. However without her I have no job. no income, no money. Currently, the state hands have not been paid for three weeks. We have no money to do it, not until performance. The money is held in trust by the theatre. If anything were to happen to her, and she did not perform, people would be given their money back and we would receive nothing."

"The opera house is in financial difficulty?" Mr Hunter frowned.

"It is not so much financial difficulty as they will only

pay if there is a performance. We might do months and months of work that we will be paid a pittance for, and on opening night we will see the large bonus. A bonus that will pay for the next few months whilst the next performance is planned and executed. But for any reason if this performance does not go ahead, we are left with nothing. We get no bonus. We must look for work elsewhere to sustain our families and ourselves. We've lost many good stage hands. I've only managed to remain due to the help of a friend," Ernest explained, looking pale.

"A wealthy friend, I trust?" Mr Hunter asked.

"He's wealthy enough. But he was a friend long before he was wealthy," Mr Boult said defensively.

"And clearly a friend long after. That is rare to find," Mr. Hunter said without any condescension.

"It is a friendship that can survive wealth," Ernest looked at Mr Hunter with a confused expression.

"A true friendship indeed," Mr Hunter agreed. "So

you have no reason to harm the signorina. In fact, it is not in your best interest at all to see her so disgraced or killed."

"No, it is, in fact, the furthest thing from my mind and I will do all I can to ensure she performs. Not only do I wish to be paid, but I want my men to be paid as well. As I'm sure you understand. Good men are hard to find these days," Mr. Bolt said.

"Is there anyone else that would wish her harm? Perhaps one of those in your company?" Mr Hunter asked.

"Who might be upset with the signorina? Aside from Miss Lind? No, none of them," Mr Boult said firmly.

"Why Miss Lind?" Alex frowned.

"She is a rising star who has performed across Europe and the signorina, well she doesn't want to be eclipsed by her. She was done all she can to ensure other sopranos can't replace her. Over the years she has been understudy on two or three operas now. And even when the signorina has been far too sick to perform or is rumoured to not be performing well enough, Miss Lind has always been fully prepared to take the stage, and that last moment been denied the opportunity. I would say that trying to stifle her career rather than allowing her to take centre stage instead is a fitting motive, don't you?" Mr Boult said.

"It is indeed," Mr. Hunter said.

"But of course, it may not be any of us," the stage manager said in and offhand manner.

"And what do you mean by that?" Mr Hunter asked.

"Well, there is always the possibility that it is not a living person behind at all. But that the theatre ghost. You have heard tales of the ghost, correct?" Mr Boult asked without a hint of irony or humour.

Mr. Hunter had to bite his lip to keep himself from laughing.

"I have not heard of any such thing," he replied honestly.

"You may scoff and mock, but in the theatre, the

supernatural is far stronger than you might expect. I would not be surprised at all to find that a ghost is behind these messages," Ernest said and had nothing further to say to Alex on the matter of the signorina, the theatre or the ghost.

Chapter 9

If the concert were to go ahead at Covent Garden, rehearsals could wait no longer. Though Lady Sarah was still suspicious of the stage manager, after her inspection of the stage with Jacques, she could see no reasons rehearsal could not take place.

The doctor agreed the signorina was well enough to rehearse, so the stage was cleared, the lights were set and the conductor and violinists took their places in the orchestra pit.

Hector sat beside Lady Sarah and Monsieur Lavingne in the front row of the audience, and Jenny Lind stood on the far side of the stage, waiting close to the wings, but in full sight of the three in the audience.

Mr. Hunter on the Baker Boys had decided that watching the rehearsal would not be the best use of their time, and set about once again combing the backstage area.

In the wake of this news of a ghost. Mr. Hunter had

decided to make a full sweep of Covent Garden to ensure

there was no such thing as the theatre ghost, or any evidence

of anything lurking there. Just superstition and gossip. Lee

and Stanley were eager to assist, not to disprove the existence

of ghosts, but because the idea of ghost hunting sounded

thrilling to the two of them than sitting through an opera.

Sylvia and Pattinson had returned to the lobby to wait

the return of the Brigadier with any news about police

assistance.

Lady Sarah was not hopeful that the brigadier would

be successful in his quest. But she knew that if anybody could

convince the chief constable to send officers on what they

deemed a wild goose chase, it was the brigadier.

It also meant that he wasn't around fussing over the

safety of all of those there.

Jacques had told Lady Sarah of the attitude the two

constables had when they been brought to the theatre, and

though she was not impressed by their attitude, she was not surprised.

The doctor had taken his fee and was preparing to depart, with a promise to return in the early evening to check on his patient.

Arwyn was stood on the stage not far from the opera singer, but far enough away to allow the soprano room to move about as she performed.

When the rehearsal began, only Mr Boult was unaccounted for. The violinist began to play and the signorina stepped forward to take centre stage.

The piece that Julio played was the main aria. Jacques noted a look of surprise on her ladyship's face when the music started.

"Is she not wearing her costume?" Lady Sarah frowned.

"Oh no, only during a full dress rehearsal with the rest of the cast and full orchestra. That only happens the night before the first performance. For now Herr Wagner and Señor Mendez needed to assess whether the signorina's voice is still able to carry the notes ahead of time. Otherwise Miss Lind will be chosen to go on instead," the theatre manager explained.

Lady Sarah set back to listen, the sound of the violin transporting her to another time and place so much so she almost forgot why she was there.

As she sat there listening, the creaking sounds of the theatre seemed to be perfectly natural. Nothing out of the ordinary.

Just as the signorina opened her mouth to sing. There was a cry from Hector as one of the sandbags was loosed from the rafters and fell right towards where the soprano was standing.

Arwyn did not miss a beat. He moved like lightning and push the signorina out of the way clear of the falling projectile.

Unfortunately for the constable, the sandbag landed on his leg, causing him to cry out in pain.

Miss Lind was staring up into the rafters trying to see if she could see anything if she could see anything up on the gangway, but there was nothing she could discern in the darkness.

Hector and the theatre manager rushed at once to the signorina who was now sobbing.

"The doctor, he has not left yet, I will go fetch him," Jacques announced as he ran off through the wings to fetch him.

Lady Sarah went to Arwyn's side. He was doing his best to not make a fuss, but it was clear to her ladyship that his leg was broken.

It did not take long for the doctor to appear with Jacques.

"Perhaps, doctor, you would be so kind as to examine the constable's leg. It is possibly a better use of your medical skills at this moment," Lady Sarah said, raising her voice to be heard above the screams of the signorina.

The doctor nodded, much to the horror of the stage manner, and went to check on Arwyn. There was nothing the doctor could do for a screaming hysterical woman. But for a broken leg and a man laying in pain, there was much more he could do.

"I shall not perform. It is too dangerous to!" Signorina Aurora cried.

"But you must you must! Come now, you are here, you have travelled all this way. To not sing for the audiences of London would be an outrage," Jacques said.

"Yes, my dear," Hector said calmly. "It is proper for you to take the stage, the show must go on, as they say."

"No, I shall not. It is just too dangerous. You have not done enough for my safety. I was nearly killed!" the opera signer screeched.

"Nearly, but not quite," Lady Sarah said pointedly.

"And what is that supposed to mean?" the signorina asked with disgust.

"That whilst you are crying over your affairs, a man is lying here in pain with a broken his leg. Something he received for saving your life, and you have yet to show him the slightest bit of gratitude," Lady Sarah retorted.

The signorina stared at her ladyship and blinked a few times, unable to find any words to say. Her eyes then slowly moved to look at the constable.

"He was just doing his job," she said with indignantly. "Pick yourself up off the floor."

She swept off to her dressing room crying crocodile tears to elicit sympathy from anyone within earshot. Lady Sarah shook her head and watched with barely concealed anger as Hector and Jacques both made to move after her.

The two men froze when they saw the look on the face of the lady and remained where they were.

"Are you quite well, constable?" Miss Lind asked as

she came to kneel by Lady Sarah.

"I am sure I will live," Arwyn said through gritted teeth.

"The actions you took to save her life. I suppose that it is all in the line of duty," Herr Bruno said as he climbed out of the orchestra pit. There was a measure of admiration in his voice.

"Protecting people from criminals is definitely within my remit. Risking my life to save people, that doesn't seem to come off that often. Though, more than you might think around Lady Sarah," Arwyn tried to smile as he winced in pain.

"Yes, it is a clean break," the doctor announced. "It will need to be splinted. You will not be able to walk for a few days. We should have you lie down until I can find something to split the leg with."

"Is there anything in the theatre we could find to use?" Lady Sarah asked.

"It is unlikely. If someone could go and fetch supplies from the hospital. That would be most helpful," the doctor replied.

"If you can tell her the way, Sylvia will gladly go, with Pattinson as her guard," Lady Sarah said. "Everyone else should remain here."

"What do you mean everyone else should remain here? Why?" the conductor demanded.

"Because now it is no longer just threats, but an attempt has been made on Signorina Aurora's life. The police cannot brush that off as mere practical jokes any more. Therefore when the Brigadier returns with assistance, they will certainly want to question everyone," Lady Sarah explained as she rose and began to move across the stage to where the stage manager was knelt.

Jacques had turned white and was shaking.

"Is everything all right?" Lady Sarah asked as she gently placed her hand upon Monsieur Lavingne's shoulder.

"I am ruined. She will not perform. It is the end of my career, and perhaps even the end of Covent Garden," Jacques sobbed.

"Come now, Miss Lind can perform," Lady Sarah soothed.

"No, you don't understand. It's all over that's the end of it all," Jacques said pitifully. Nothing else Lady Sarah said could elicit a different answer from the theatre manager.

It was clear that the theatre manager was in a greater state of shock than the signorina, and the doctor prescribed a sedative for the man, then had to lead Jacques to his office to lay down for a while.

Moments later Mr Hunter and the Baker Boys arrived on the scene.

"Well, we certainly have missed a lot of excitement," Mr Hunter sighed as he surveyed the state of the stage.

"I think Lee and Stanley should do some climbing into those rafters," Lady Sarah said quietly as she approached

Alex. "See what they can find. Something may have been left behind by the person who loosed the sandbag."

"Whatever you wish. Who was unaccounted for at the time?" Mr Hunter asked.

"Mr Boult was the only one absent, and the three of you. Everyone else I can be relatively certain of where they were," Lady Sarah said.

"That somewhat shortens our list of suspects." Mr Hunter sighed.

"Potentially. But it depends on what the Baker boys find," Lady Sarah replied.

"Stanley and Lee, to the gangway," Mr Hunter announced. The two boys leapt at the chance to go climbing above the stage. The two scrambled away and fought about who would be the first to reach the precarious ledge that hung over the stage.

The gangway was little more than a piece of wood, suspended on wires that hung above the stage with rope ladders at either end as the access points.

The scenery and sandbags were all tied to close to the gangway, so that they could be raised and lowered as needed. The sandbags were used as counterweights and did not easily come loose, unless they were untied.

The stage hands would also watch the performances from the gangway, with a different vantage point than those below.

To work in that space, you had to be light and fearless. To fall from that height was almost certain death, but this did not occur to Lee or Stanley as they climbed to the towering heights above. They carefully made their way across the gangway crawling to avoid shaking it too badly when they reached the point where the sandbag had fallen from.

When the pair reached the point above where Constable Evans was still lying, it was easy to see that the someone had intentionally cut the rope. The cut ran all the way through the rope, without a single frayed strand. For this to be cut so cleanly, it had to be done in real time, not simply left to hang and possibly fall at an opportune moment.

But this was not something that had yet occurred to the two boys. They merely assessed the rope, saw that had been cut, and started looking around for anything that looked out of place.

"What can you see?" Lady Sarah called up.

"The rope's been cut," Stanley called back.

"Cut not worn through?" Lady Sarah asked.

"How could we tell?" Lee yelled.

" If the rope has frayed, there will be lots of strands that have pulled to very thin ends .If the rope has been cut it will have a smooth finish," Lady Sarah said, before she moved over to where the sandbag lay and suddenly took hold of the end of it.

"It looks smooth," Stanley replied

"Yes, I would agree," Lady Sarah said. "This must have been cut with something very sharp. Who would have a knife that sharp in a theatre?" she wondered.

"Because I feel like you may arrive at the answer before I tell you this is," Hector sighed, "Mr Boult has such a knife. As the stage manager, he often has to be quick to deal with any problems during a performance, including keeping the stage clear. Should anything become wrapped or tangled, he must be able to cut it before anyone knew there was a problem." the actor said

"Well, then Mr Boult becomes more and more suspicious. Has anybody seen him recently?" Lady Sarah asked as she let go of the rope.

"No, not since you were asking us questions earlier. When he was with me. I do not know what happened to him after he left me."

"The last I saw of him was before that," Lady Sarah said thoughtfully.

"The doctor will be with the signorina by now, so for the moment she does not need a new bodyguard. But do you really think that Mr Boult is behind the threats and the attempt on her life?" Mr Hunter asked in a low voice.

"I can't say for certain," Lady Sarah said. "But it does look that way."

"I found it!" the voice of Lee called out a moment later.

"You found what?" Lady Sarah called back.

"We found the knife!" Stanley said, leaning slightly too far off the gangway so that Lee had to grab hold of him to keep his brother from falling.

"Come down, the pair of you. Bring the knife with you," Lady Sarah said as she shook her head.

"They are very keen investigators but they have much to learn about their own self preservation," Mr Hunter chuckled.

Jacques was sedated and lying down in the ticket office, so he was in no shape to answer a question about the knife.

Though Hector had known about the existence of the Mr Boult's knife, he as an actor, did not know what it would look like, nor did Miss Lind.

The conductor and violinist we're no longer talking to Lady Sarah after being sequestered in the theatre. And so the only thing that that remained to do was to find Mr Boult.

Chapter 10

The search for Mr Boult began in earnest. Mr Jamieson had to locate the spare set of keys for the theatre for Lady Sarah so she might open every single door possible.

Sylvia and Pattinson had left upon the doctor's request and would return as they possibly could. In the meantime, Arwyn had no choice but to wait on the stage, doing his best to keep his eyes and ears open despite the pain. The constable as beginning to resent his assignment, and Captain Jonnes Smith for giving it to him.

But even with his broken leg, he was secure in the knowledge that at least he was not abandoning his post.

Lady Sarah, however, would not stand by whilst Mr Hunter and the two Baker Boys conducted their search for the missing stage manager.

The brigadier had returned with promises of at least

one officer arriving within the hour from the chief constable

and replaced Arwyn as the signorina's bodyguard. When

Sylvia and Pattinson returned from the hospital with the

items the doctor required, Arwyn's leg was splintered and he

was taken to share the guarding duties with the brigadier.

This allowed the brigadier some time to be told of all

that had happened in his absence, whilst the signorina was

sedated as heavily as the theatre manager was.

Sylvia and Pattinson sat in guarded the front doors of

the theatre. The doors had been bolted with instructions that

no one was to leave, and none of those held captive inside the

theatre wanted to test Pattinson's resolve as a guard dog.

Lady Sarah had also decided to ensure that the back

doors were locked as well. The only other person with the key

to the back door was Mr Boult. But after the sandbag incident,

Lady Sarah knew he had not left the premises just yet.

She given Sylvia instructions that when the policeman

arrived, he was to be in, but no one but still no one was to leave.

Mr Jamieson and Miss Lind stayed with Sylvia as much to stay in a position where they would know they could leave as soon as possible, but to keep watch over Jacques as the entrance to the ticket office was in the foyer.

Herr Wagner and Señor Mendez rehearsed in the upper circle where they could be heard the whole time by Silvia. She felt it was a lot like babysitting, but she was not keen to be involved in investigating this mystery. The rumour of the ghost and with what had happened to Constable Evans, she was very glad to simply sit and make sure nobody left.

The search of the theatre was conducted in a regimented manner. The four began by the back door to the theatre, and worked towards the stage and beyond.

Lee and Stanley Baker were sent up into the rafters and then down into the small areas where only they could squeeze.

Mr Hunter refused to leave Lady Sarah on her own. So the pair made a comprehensive sweep of all the dressing rooms, storerooms, and even the bathrooms to ensure that wherever Mr Boult was hiding he would be found.

It was the third storeroom, one that was filled with broken ends of old chairs, old rows, broken fixtures from around the theatre, that they finally came across Mr Boult.

He was lying, unconscious, buried beneath a pile of the chair legs. At a first glance, the couple could see nothing in the room. But as they were conducting such a thorough search, it did not take long for them to discover him.

"It does not look much like he was trying to hide," Mr Hunter said with a frown on his face.

"No, indeed not. It looks like he was put in here. We should fetch the doctor," Lady Sarah said firmly. They removed all the chair legs that had been burying him. Push them to one side, Mr Hunter picked up the unconscious stage manager and carried him to one of the empty dressing rooms as Lady Sarah went to summon the doctor.

As Mr Boult was the one they believed to be responsible for the sandbag incident, Mr Hunter did not want him in the same room as the signorina for the moment.

The doctor seemed be less than impressed at the number of injuries that were stacking up in the theatre, but he came despite his ill-humour.

It took smelling salts to bring Mr Boult back to a conscious state, and after making sure nothing was broken and that it was just a bump on the head; the doctor was satisfied that the stage manager would recover with a small amount of rest

"Mr Boult, we need to ask you some questions," Lady Sarah said once the doctor had left the room. Her serious tone and the cold look upon her face were enough to send the stage manager into a state of mild panic.

"What's happened? Why are you talking to me? Why am I in here?" Mr Boult asked, very clearly somewhat disoriented.

"We found you, Ernest, buried underneath broken pieces of the old chairs from the stalls in one of the storerooms. What is the last thing you remember?" Lady Sarah asked more gently than she had intended.

"I do not know. I was on my way to meet someone. And then I was here," Mr Boult said with confusion as he reached up to touch his head. He winced in pain and instant regret, and felt a wave of nausea threaten to overwhelm him.

"Who were you going to meet?" Mr Hunter asked with suspicion.

"That is none of your business!" Mr Boult snapped.

"A romantic meeting?" Lady Sarah asked.

"Perhaps, perhaps not," Ernest said.

"I understand," Lady Sarah said as she leaned back on the small stool she was sat upon. "Mr Boult, someone attempted to kill the signorina during the on stage rehearsal. The only person that is unaccounted for during that time is you. We found your knife up on the gangway. Can you explain that?"

Lady Sarah was looking at him with a steady gaze. There was no condemnation and no accusation in her look, but Mr Boult instantly stiffened.

"You think I'm the one behind all this? Of course you do. Of course it has to be me. Always the stage manager," he said shaking his head. "Always that low, poor person responsible for wanting the rich, horrible ones out of the way. Well, it wasn't me. Wasn't near the stage. You found me in a storeroom? I don't even know how long it's been since I was meant to meet this person," Mr Boult said acidly.

"Is that your last word on the matter?" Lady Sarah asked.

"It is. Now leave me. I want to get some rest," Mr Boult said.

Mr Hunter opened his mouth about to suggest that perhaps he should try to stay awake with a head injury. But

Lady Sarah shook her head at him. When a man was stubborn like Mr Boult even the best advice would be ignored.

"Well, where does that leave us?" Mr Hunter asked as he shut the door to the dressing room that Mr Boult was lying in.

"It leaves us without a suspect," Lady Sarah sighed and lapsed into silence as she thought.

"It leaves us with a ghost," Mr Hunter said flatly.

"It leaves us with a ghost," Lady Sarah sighed.

"Lady Sarah! Lady Sarah! Lady Sarah!" the Baker boys voiced echoed down the corridor to the couple's ears as the two boys came running up to meet Mr Hunter and Lady Sarah.

"What is it boys?" Lady Sarah asked with curiosity.

"That hiding place we found amongst all that scenery. It's not there any more! Everything's gone!" Lee said.

"Everything?" Lady Sarah frowned.

"Yes, all of it!" Stanley said.

"Show me," Mr Hunter insisted.

"I will see you all back in the foyer," Lady Sarah said and walked off to circle the stalls as she thought.

"Be careful," Mr Hunter said gently.

"You too," Lady Sarah replied.

Chapter 11

Mr Jamieson slipped out of the theatre foyer and went to find Lady Sarah with a worried expression on his face. He seemed to be rather agitated when he spied her ladyship in the auditorium.

"Can I speak to you privately?" he asked in a low voice. He knew that voices, even in the stalls could carry quite easily to the circle, and though the conductor and violinists were rehearsing now, there was no telling when they may decide to stop and take a break.

"Very well. Where would be best?" Lady Sarah asked.

"Perhaps in one of the empty dressing rooms," Hector said. Lady Sarah nodded and followed in the direction that the actor led. There could be something said for following a suspect, alone, into a dressing room at the far end of the theatre, but Lady Sarah was not worried.

Of all those to suspect that might have a cause to harm her, Hector was at the bottom of her list.

"Have you found Mr Boult yet?" Mr Jamieson asked tentatively.

"Yes, we have," Lady Sarah replied slowly.

"Where is he?" Hector asked with rising note of worry.

"In one of the dressing rooms. Resting," her ladyship said, eyeing the actor with caution.

"Why? What happened?" Mr Jamieson asked with a terrified look in his eyes.

"He was supposedly knocked unconscious and then buried under some chair legs in one of the storage rooms," Lady Sarah replied.

"Supposedly? you don't believe him?" Mr Jamieson asked.

"That remains to be seen," Lady Sarah shrugged.

"I know you suspect him. You found that knife on the

gangway. It was his. I know I said that I did not recognise it, but I did. I couldn't tell you that it was his without incriminating him. But I know he was never anywhere near that. He was supposed to be-" Mr Jamieson said and his voice trailed off.

"Supposed to be where?" Lady Sarah asked with a raised eyebrow.

"My lady, what I'm about to tell you is known by very few. And those that do know are sworn to absolute secrecy. In telling you this, I trust that it will go no further. Not even to that of your fiancé," Mr Jamieson said seriously, all pretences had been dropped. All manner of the masks he normally worn had fallen away.

He stood looking very vulnerable by the full-length dressing room mirror.

"Very well. Whatever you tell me now shall not pass my lips," Lady Sarah agreed solemnly.

"Mr Boult was supposed to be meeting with me.

We've been lovers for many, many years, secretly as you can imagine. My predilections are not widely accepted, nor celebrated by any of those outside of a very select few," Mr Jamieson said tactfully.

"I see. So when Mr Boult talked about retirement, and a new life, with a friend with money," Lady Sarah started.

"Yes. He was talking about me. We have plans to leave, to go far away. Where we can live as we will," Hector said wistfully.

"Where would you go?" Lady Sarah asked.

"Perhaps as far as New Zealand or Australia, there's a great amount of space there. You can live a very solitary life while still being part of a community and they will almost know nothing of your lives together," Mr. Jamieson says quite sadly.

"But you will miss the theatre. You will miss society," Lady Sarah protested.

"There is society to be found anywhere that humans

have gone. But I will miss the theatre. I will miss the London

Theatre," Mr. Jamieson sighed. "But for the sake of the man

that I love, and the life that we wish to leave, I will sacrifice

it," Mr Jamieson said with finality.

"Then how was it that you became engaged to the

signorina?" Lady Sarah asked.

"Now there is a tale," Mr Jamieson said. "I was of

course trying to hide my true nature, to blend with the

expected norms and behaviour of our crowd. When Aurora

discovered my true desires, it was the night before the

wedding. I found that I couldn't go through with the

wedding. It was I who broke the engagement. But to allow

her to save face, we decided to say that it was because of her

career. Yes, her career was blossoming and growing.

"She may well have left me for that very reason, given

time, but though people asking questions about why a young

strapping man in the theatre was not playing, flirting or

engaging in debauchery, should I say, with the lower female

orders. It was unthinkable. Before Aurora, people had begun to ask questions and were getting too close to knowing the truth. I convinced the   signorina that I was the suitor she had always desired. Part of a dutiful and loving couple that we were intending to get married, and I would continue my life with Ernest in secret."

"But you did come to love her in a fashion. So much so, you could not go through with a wedding," Lady Sarah said.

"No, It was too much guilt, and too much for Ernest. He didn't mind a false pretence of wooing and seducing, but the idea that we would have to officially be married living together living under that roof was too distasteful for him. He also thought it was unfair to Aurora, if you can believe that," Hector said.

"I can believe it well enough. You have both had much to lose, and good reason to guard your secret. I am sure that you did not intend to hurt anybody," Lady Sarah said kindly.

"There was no intent, but even so Aurora was very hurt when I told her, and extremely embarrassed. It was for the best in the end. We've both been much happier since then," Hector said with a smile curling at the corner of his mouth.

"And how have you covered your tracks in the meantime?" Lady Sarah asked with curiosity.

"Well, when you get a woman drunk enough, she can believe that she has been seduced. Even if all that has happened is that you have put her in her bed, lying beside her until she has fallen asleep and then crawled away," Mr Jamieson sighed.

"Adept at deception, though I should say that is not too kind a reflection on most women," Lady Sarah said.

"Perhaps, but I do not wish to waste your time, my lady, which I know is very valuable. I did not wish you to keep going on this rather wild goose chase. Ernest has never borne any ill will towards the signorina. In fact he has done everything he can to defend her and to make sure she is happy. Simply to apologise for all that I did to her," Hector said.

"Thank you. I appreciate all you have told me," Lady Sarah said with gratitude.

"May I see him now?" Hector asked with a note of worry.

"Of course," Lady Sarah said and she led Mr Jamieson off to the room in which Mr Boult was resting. Ernest was extremely happy to see Hector, and as the pair settled down to talk, Lady Sarah shut the door and locked it. There was no reason for the pair to be disturbed, and after all she had learnt, she was certain the pair would be safer behind a locked door.

Chapter 12

Mr Hunter and the Baker Boys soon returned from the backstage and met Lady Sarah in the auditorium.

"They are right. Everything was gone," Mr Hunter said simply.

"I suspected as much," Lady Sarah said with an odd expression on her face.

"What do you mean?" Mr Hunter asked. "I thought Mr Boult was your favoured suspect."

"No, not any more. There are mitigating circumstances," Lady Sarah said delicately.

"I see," Mr. Hunter said. "Where is he now?"

"He and Mr Jamieson are speaking in the dressing room," Lady Sarah said.

"So you don't suspect either of the gentleman?" Mr Hunter asked with exasperation.

"No. No, they're not responsible for any attack on the signorina. In fact, they have no reason to harm her at all, and she has every reason to harm them. In fact, I would go so far as to say that none of our suspects have any reason to harm her. Yet her motives to destroy them are much stronger," Lady Sarah said and bit her lower lip.

"Then who is responsible? Who cut the sandbag? Who tried to kill her? Who left those messages?" Mr Hunter asked.

"It must be the ghost then," Lee said simply with a shrug.

"Yes, the ghost took away all the clothes and the things from that little shelter and the ghost is the one who cut the rope and wrote the messages," Stanley agreed.

"Though, may not be a ghost, I would agree that the same person is responsible for all of those things," Lady Sarah said. "I just do not know if it is possible," she mused a moment or two.

Her thoughts were interrupted though as the door to

the auditorium was thrown open, and Sylvia stepped through

with a constable beside her.

"I see my father was successful," Mr Hunter said with

a mild amount of admiration.

"Indeed he was. This is Constable Giles. He will be

assisting us in this investigation," Sylvia said.

"Well, perhaps assisting in the arrest. I believe the

investigation is all but over. Perhaps you might be so good as

to sit down and listen to see whether you agree with our

findings," Lady Sarah said

"Your findings," Mr. Hunter said proudly.

"So you believe you've already solved this sorry state

of affairs?" Sylvia asked as she settled into one of the front

row seats.

"I believe that we should send Pattinson to watch over

the signorina and bring the brigadier and Arwyn to listen too.

They will want to hear all of this, and I suspect that they will

have some extra insight. Sylvia, why would you be so good as to deliver Pattinson and bring our friends back with you?" Lady Sarah asked.

"Of course," Sylvia agreed. She stood and walked back to the foyer to fetch the dog, and then on to the dressing rooms to do as Lady Sarah asked.

"Is there a reason that you wanted her to do this now?" Mr Hunter asked.

"Perhaps," Lady Sarah replied quietly.

"I see. Then we will just have to wait," Mr Hunter replied.

"It should not be too long," Lady Sarah smiled. The Baker boys collapsed into the chairs in the stalls and the group lapsed into silence and listened.

Constable Giles looked very confused as to why they were waiting, but a few moments later the sound of the dog barking could be heard.

This was followed by doors being flung open and tried to be shut behind them.

"Your missing piece of the puzzle?" the constable

reasoned.

"I believe it is," Lady Sarah smiled.

"Do you know the direction that noise is coming from

and how to get there?" the constable asked.

"We do! We know a shortcut! Come this way,"

Stanley announced and Lee nodded. The two boys set off at a

run, with Mr Hunter running after them. Lady Sarah and

Constable Giles followed at a much more sedate pace.

"Will you not lose sight of them if we are not quick?"

the constable asked.

"Mr Hunter is more than able to keep up with that

pair of troublemakers, and I think you'll agree, Constable

Giles, that it is not suitable for a lady to run in such a

beautiful and illustrious place," Lady Sarah said with a smile.

Constable Giles frowned, unsure what to make of the

situation, but decided that running after Mr Hunter and the

two Baker Boys was better than listening to Lady Sarah speak in riddles.

As the constable followed in pursuit, there was a sound of a scuffle; of growling and a shriek. The two Baker boys, Mr Hunter and the constable came across a woman lying on the ground with Patterson pulling at her clothing.

"Get it off get it off now," the woman cried.

Mr Hunter was dumbstruck as he recognised the woman laying on the ground, and was uncertain how on earth she got there.

Chapter 13

When Sylvia was still at the dressing room door Pattinson had taken off at a great rate chasing after a phantom. The doctor and the signorina were still both in the dressing room.

They heard the shriek of the girl, and all the colour drained from the signorina's face. She tried to stand up, the doctor pushed her down. And when she tried to force her way past the doctor, Sylvia, the brigadier, and Constable Evans blocked the doorway.

"I believe, Constable Evans, that the lady will have to come with you," the brigadier said grimly.

"Where are we taking her?" Arwyn asked.

"To the foyer. Lady Sarah will be there with the others, and our doctor, if you would you be so good as to join us. I can escort the soprano, if Sylvia, you and the doctor would be so kind as to help Arwyn. I believe that the theatre

is now safe," the brigadier said as he took hold of Aurora's

arm and escorted her to the front of the opera house.

Jacques had come around nicely and was no longer

feeling the ill effects of his panic attack. He lay sprawled

across one of the sofas, but still present for what was about to

happen. Lady Sarah had fetched Mr Boult and Mr Jamieson

from the dressing room and prepared another sofa for the

injured man to lie upon.

All were assembled to listen to the solution to the

mystery that had plagued the opera house.

"It is so wonderful that we have managed to bring

you all here together, and that no one died during this terrible

ordeal. I know the signorina herself is pleased to have

survived such a frightening situation. Perhaps she would be

so good as to favour us with a song to thank us, and

celebrate," Lady Sarah said. Everyone assembled exchanged

confused looks, the   signorina, however, looked white as a

sheet, and just shook her head.

"Is there a reason you do not want to sing, signorina?" Lady Sarah asked innocently.

"I am saving my voice," the singer said flatly.

"Come now, that is not true. In fact, I would go so far as to say that that is a lie," Lady Sarah replied.

"How dare you!" the soprano tried to sound offended at such a suggestion, but her voice wavered as she spoke. "Everyone here is acquainted with Aurora Ricci, prima donna soprano, opera singer supreme and knows she does not lie," the signorina said with a measure of arrogance to her voice.

"But are you Aurora Ricci? Because to my eyes, this is Aurora Ricci," Lady Sarah said as turned slightly to indicate the doors to the auditorium as they opened. Through them, the Baker boys and Pattinson marched with a woman who was the spitting image of the opera singer.

"Or is it perhaps, a family resemblance?" Lady Sarah asked.

The looks on the faces on each of those gathered

registered nothing but shock.

"How can you possibly be alive? You were killed after

drinking that-" Herr Wagner said, his voice trailing off unable

to finish his sentence. "I see. Not dead at all. But you did not

want to marry me," Bruno said sadly.

"No, no, that is not it, Bruno," the supposed soprano

protested.

"Quite, you fool! I am Aurora Ricci, and yes, we did

this because every single person in this room slighted us and

tried to destroy our lives. Did you know that it was Jacques

that made the concoction that my sister drank. I destroyed her

voice because he knew only one of us would make it. As a

soprano, there could not be two two singers that looked alike.

And he had invested heavily in my career. Not in hers,"

Aurora said bitterly as she tried to shake the hands of the two

Baker boys from her. Pattinson growled and she halted her

attempts to escape.

"May I ask your name?" Lady Sarah said only to the sister. She shook her head and remained silent with a look of terror on her face.

"Her name is Isabella. Isabella Ricci," Bruno said looking close to tears.

"Do you believe what your sister says, that it was Monsieur Lavingne who tried to destroy your voice?" Lady Sarah asked.

"Of course. Who else would have anything to gain from such an act?" Isabella asked innocently.

"Your sister," Lady Sarah said simply.

"How dare you accuse me of such a thing!" Aurora roared.

"Quiet, woman. We have had enough from you for now," the Brigadier growled. "Please continue, my dear," he said turning back to Lady Sarah.

"This was an interesting investigation, one I might say that brought up more secrets and buried history than I thought possible in such a place but it all comes down to one thing. Singing operas and success. The signorina here was slighted by Hector Jamieson, when he left her at the altar. It was not her that abandoned him, but he who abandoned her, and allowed the world to believe that it was her career blossoming that led to his departure," Lady Sarah explained.

"She would have us believe that Mr Boult has a vendetta against her. But that is not true. Mr Boult has done everything in his power to take care of, and indeed make the signorina comfortable. If he were indeed trying to kill her, he would have had ample opportunity. A man so devoted to a singer in such a way could not possibly be the one writing such terrible messages. Besides he was attacked and thrown into a storeroom, buried beneath broken chair legs and left to die. If we had not found him when we did, I am sure the doctor would agree, that would have been the end of Mr Boult, and only someone with a vendetta against the man could do such a thing.

"Signorina, I know your motivations in that case. They are not motivations that I will make public. But I have no doubt that you are guilty of trying to kill the poor man. Now as far as Herr Wagner is concerned, he was a world famous conductor, who did not have eyes for you, but for your sister. A man, who for all intents and purposes, would have taken your sister on a most advantageous career trajectory. To marry a composer and having him write for you is an exceedingly advantageous situation to find yourself in. One that you will extremely jealous of. Is that not so?" Lady Sarah asked.

"He is not a composer, he is a conductor," Aurora spat.

"I think that you shall find that he is indeed a composer, and you know full well, that he has written and composed some most beautiful works. It is jealousy that drove you to create the concoction your sister drank and pass it off as the work of Monsieur Lavingne to mask your attempt to kill your own sister, especially when she survived, that you did not expect. But her voice is entirely ruined, and she could not face the world that believed her dead. In fact, you convinced her that she was safer with everyone believing she was dead, and that was there was only you who could protect her.

"My dear Isabella, you have lived in the shadow of your sister for so many years, and she is the one who put you there. Her desire, her need for control and power, is the reason for it. As for Monsieur Lavingne, we are told he idolised your sister, but he thought you was a far superior singer. Is that not so?" Lady Sarah asked, turning to the theatre manager.

"It is. I did not like to speak out of turn before. When you have a prima donna performing at your opera house, it is in very bad taste to talk of how much better her sister was, but she was truly spectacular. A great talent that never was given a true chance. And Miss Lind is the same. Miss Lind has the same magic, the same fire that Isabella had when she

sang. Something that Aurora's performances are severely

lacking," Jacques agreed as he looked at Isabella with

wonder.

"Were you going to replace the signorina, or rather

Aurora, with Miss Lind and give her the opportunity to stand

centre stage," Lady Sarah asked.

"Yes, I suppose that there is no hiding that when a

great talent when it is in front of you. I am sure in your

conversations with Miss Lind she did not mention it. But you

seem to be an excellent judge of character in such situations,

your ladyship. It is unsurprising to me that you were to learn

of these things," Jacques said as he hung his headset slightly.

"So the mastermind behind all these attacks. The one

committing all these attacks, was the signorina herself?" Julio

asked with a slightly stilted accent.

"Yes. But what is even more insidious is that when

she cut the sandbag, she was trying to kill her sister. A

moment of jealousy, of old wounds being ripped open when she saw Isabella standing on that stage. If she had been successful, it would have caused far more problems for her. She would have been able to return to the stage without crying imposter. Then she would have to face all sorts of questions about what had really happened to her sister. It was this mistake that led to her becoming a suspect," Lady Sarah said.

"There was no way Mr Boult could have been in the rafters at the time, and she left evidence to implicate him. She had already dispatched him and locked him away, hoping that no one would find him," Lady Sarah explained.

"You have ruined everything. Why did you have to get involved?" the signorina spat.

"You brought me here. You invited us here. You came running to our household begging for shelter. Perhaps in future you should know more about the reputations of those that you would try to use in your schemes as witnesses,"

Lady Sarah said candidly.

"Signorina Aurora Ricci, you are under arrest. Charged with vandalism, attempted murder and I am sure there are many other charges that will be levied against you as soon as my superiors here all that her ladyship has to say," Constable Giles said with a measure of respect for Lady Sarah.

"What are we to do? What can save this performance now" Jacques asked, his head in his hands as he watched the signorina being taken from the theatre.

"Well, Miss Lind, I believe is ready to perform. And there is scandal. My dear monsieur, scandal is a great way to fill a theatre," the brigadier grinned.

"Yes," Isabella said, "We could tell them all the tale of of my terrible sister of all she tried to do. Bruno, we could write that opera together. Something for Miss Linda sing perhaps," Isabella said with a smile and hope in her voice.

Bruno looked over at his former fiancée and for a

moment, it seemed like he would turn and walk away. But the sheer emotion and relief that registered on his face caused him to rush and embrace the woman that he had once been so ready to marry.

"Oh my love, I have missed you so," Bruno cried.

"We are together again. Nothing will part us this time, I swear it," Isabella promised.

The theatre that evening was a sold out performance that not a soul dared to miss. There was not a seat spare in the whole house, and people were lining the street outside just in case a seat were to be vacated.

Lady Sarah, the brigadier, Sylvia, Mr Hunter, Constable Evans, Lee and Stanley were given a box to sit and watch the performance from. It was Lee and Stanley's first opera, and to hear Miss Lind sing was a true delight for them both. They say that opera is something that you can learn to appreciate if you do not love it the first time that you hear it, but for Lee and Stanley opera was already part of their souls, so moved were they by every moment.

It was a thrilling evening for all, and a most triumphant début for Miss Lind.

Love the book? Need to know what's next in Stickleback Hollow?

The stakes couldn't be higher at Ascot. A new stand has just been opened, but under the pageantry and celebration lurks a dark secret. Beneath the thunder of horses' hooves and the roar of the crowd, can a murder really be hiding?

Get A Day at the Races now!

Want to stay up to date with all the latest news from Stickleback Hollow, then you can sign up to my Stickleback Hollow Ream Community, you can **follow** the Ream completely free and get access to updates, news and lots of cool things you can't get anywhere else! Sign up here.

Looking for more than just books? You can get the latest releases from me, signed paperbacks and hardbacks, mugs, t-shirts, journals as well as books and digital bundles from

https://www.cswoolley.com

Love the Mysteries of Stickleback Hollow? Not caught up with the rest of the series, then jump back to *A Thief in Stickleback Hollow*, Book 1 in the Mysteries of Stickleback Hollow and see how it all began.

Want to help a reader out? Reviews are crucial when it comes to helping readers choose their next book and you can help them by leaving just a few sentences about this book as a review. It doesn't have to be anything fancy, just what you liked about the book and who you think might like to read it.

Scan the QR Code below or visit

https://mybook.to/ANightAtTheOpera.

If you don't have time to leave a review or don't feel

confident writing one, recommending a book to your family,

friends and co-workers can help them choose their next book,

so feel free to spread the word.

Chapter 8

"Non vedo l'ora di sentirti cantare. Ho sentito molte cose su di te,"

"I can't wait to hear you sing. I have heard a lot about you,"

"Oh che meraviglia ascoltare la mia lingua qui."

"Oh how wonderful to hear my language here."

"Ma tu hai un bel cuore. Fare un gesto del genere mi ha fatto sentire un po' meno la mancanza della mia patria,"

"But you have a beautiful heart. To make such a gesture has made me miss my homeland just a little less,"

Chapter 8

"¿Por qué estás aquí ahora? Seguramente sólo el director de orquesta, la prima donna y el director del teatro son requeridos tan temprano antes de la representación."

"Why is it that you are here now? Surely only the conductor, prima donna, and theatre manager are required so early before the performance."

"Hace mucho tiempo que no va al teatro, ni siquiera a la ópera. En una representación hay muchas partes en movimiento. Aunque antes era costumbre que sólo se llamara a unos pocos a la vez. Ahora es imperativo que estemos tantos juntos para que podamos actuar cohesionados. La Signora cantará sobre mi violín, aumentando su tono para sobrepasar mis notas, es algo que debo saber. Hay momentos en los que tendré que tocar más bajo. Igualmente hay momentos en los que, si la signorina no puede alcanzar una determinada nota, puede que tenga que tocar más alto para cubrir su carencia. No puedo descubrir esto sin estar aquí en los ensayos sin su voz,"

"It's been a long time since you have been to the theatre or even an opera house. In a performance, there are many moving parts. Although it used to be custom that only a few were called at a time. It is now imperative that we have so many of us together so that we may perform cohesively. The Signora will sing over my violin, increasing her pitch to overpower my notes, it is something I must know. There are times I will have to play more quietly. Equally there are moments where, if the signorina cannot reach a certain note, I may have to play louder to cover for her shortfall. I cannot discover this without being here at rehearsals without her voice,"

"Ya veo. Esto es algo en lo que nunca había pensado. Pero usted ha tocado en un gran número de locales impresionantes. ¿Habrás actuado antes con la signorina?"

"I see. This is something I had never thought about before. But you have played in a great number of impressive venues. You must have performed with the signorina before?"

"No he tocado antes con ella, pero la he visto actuar. Era mucho más joven entonces, su voz ha madurado con ella, pero a medida que una voz madura, se hace más difícil tocar ciertas notas. La voz se desgasta como las cuerdas de un violín,"

"I have not played with her before, but I have seen her perform. She was much younger then, her voice has matured with her, but as a voice matures, it becomes harder for certain notes to be hit. The voice wears out much like the strings of a violin,"

"Bueno, una cuerda de violín se puede sustituir, pero

una voz, sin embargo, es un poco más difícil de reemplazar,"

"Well a violin string can be replaced, but a voice, however, that is a little harder to replace,"

"Estoy seguro de que en esto, la signorina estaría de acuerdo,"

"I'm sure in this, the signorina would agree,"

"Puedo entender entonces por qué usted, y la señorita Lind, estarían ambos aquí, ella debe conocer los entresijos de la actuación si tiene que cubrir a una signorina enferma o si la signorina no puede actuar por cualquier razón. Pero, ¿y el actor? Seguramente no hay necesidad de que esté aquí,"

"I can understand then why you, and Miss Lind, would both be here, she must know the ins and outs of the performance if she has to cover for a sick signorina or if the signorina should not be able to perform for any reason. But what of the actor? Surely there's no need for him to be here,"

"A esta ópera en particular se le ha añadido un papel específicamente para Héctor. Está terminando su carrera. Es su último hurra, como podría decirse, su canto del cisne. Así que tiene un papel sin canto para despedirse del público de Londres. Vamos a recorrer el resto de Europa y a despedirnos en su nombre de los demás escenarios. Tiene un gran talento que echaremos mucho de menos,"

"This particular opera has had a role added to it specifically for Hector. He is finishing his career. It is his last hurrah, as you might say, his swan song. So he has a non-singing walk-on part to say farewell to the audiences of London. We are going to tour the rest of Europe and say goodbye on his behalf to the other stages. He has a great talent that will be sadly missed,"

"¿Por qué se retira?"

"Why is it he is retiring?"

"Nadie lo sabe con certeza. No ha dicho nada ni ha confirmado o desmentido ningún rumor,"

"No one quite knows for sure. He has not said anything nor confirmed or denied any rumours,"

"¿Cómo puedes estar seguro de que este es su último hurra como dices?"

"How can you be sure this is his last hurrah as you say?"

"En realidad es simple. Le oí discutir con Monsieur Lavingne sobre su futuro,"

"It is simple really. I heard him arguing with Monsieur Lavingne about his future,"

"Pero, ¿por qué ahora?"

"But why now?"

"Tiene algo que ver con la signorina; alguna forma de secreto. No he oído nada más que eso,"

"It has something to do with the signorina; some form of secret. I heard nothing more than that,"

"Ya veo. ¿Así que crees que Héctor tiene motivos más que suficientes para querer hacerle daño?"

"I see. So you feel that Hector has more than a good enough motive for wanting to harm her?"

"Posiblemente, pero no más que cualquiera de los presentes, yo incluido,"

"Possibly, but no more than anyone else here, myself included,"

"¿Y por qué tienes una vendetta contra ella?"

"And why would you have a vendetta against her?"

"¿Yo? Bueno, eso es fácil. No quería que actuara con ella. Se empeñó en elegir a otro violinista. Un violinista de segunda con el que aparentemente tuvo un tumultuoso romance en muchas ocasiones, especialmente durante el tiempo en que supuestamente tuvo una relación con el Sr. Jamieson,"

"Me? Well, that is easy. She did not want me to perform with her. She was adamant that some other violinist would be chosen. A second rate fiddler that she has apparently had a tumultuous affair with on many occasions especially during the time she was supposedly in a relationship with Mr Jamieson,"

"Entonces tiene un motivo aún mayor para querer hacerle daño,"

"Then he has an even greater motive for wanting to harm her,"

"En efecto, pero Monsieur Lavingne se mantuvo firme y se aseguró de que me contrataran. Creo que era Herr Bruno quien me quería aquí más que nadie,"

"Indeed, but Monsieur Lavingne stood firm and it made sure that I was hired. I believe it was Herr Bruno who wanted me here more than anyone else,"

Historical Note

Covent Garden has been a site for a total of three theatres. It currently is the home of the Royal Opera House, which opened in 1860, but the first theatre opened there in 1728, when John Rich, the actor/manager at Lincoln's Inn Fields, commissioned an opera entitled *The Beggar's Opera*.

For the first hundred years of it's history, Covent Garden was mostly a playhouse, and was one of the two playhouses that were granted Letters of Patent by Charles II. Covent Garden and Drury Lane had almost sole rights for all spoken dramas performed in London.

The first serious works performed at Covent Garden were the operas of Handel. From 1735 until his death in 1759, there were regular seasons of Handel that were performed, some of which were written by Handel for those performances.

In 1808, a fire destroyed the original Covent Garden Theatre. Handel's organ which was bequeathed to John Rich, was lost during this fire, along with many other valuable items.

Rebuilding the theatre began at once, and the second Theatre Royal at Covent Garden opened on 18th September 1809. It is in this theatre that our mystery is set. Though it did not truly become an opera house until 1847 after it was remodelled, for the sake of dramatic license and to serve the story, I moved the remodel to a slightly earlier time frame.

In 1856, the second disaster at Covent Garden happened. Another fire destroyed the theatre completely. The rebuild of the theatre was delayed by finances, but it was completed and opened in 1858. Then in 1892, it became the Royal Opera House that we know today.

Miss Jenny Lind is the only one of the characters in this book that actually live. She was a soprano who found notoriety during the 1800s. Known as the Swedish Nightingale, she was born in 1820, and found fame in 1838 when performing in Sweden. To have her touring opera houses outside of Sweden for experience in the 1830s would not be too out of the question.

Opera is something this is a little different when it comes to the role of a director. If you are unfamiliar with opera, you might have been surprised at the lack of a director in this story. However, the director of an opera is known as a producer. In the case of this book, Herr Bruno and Jacques

Lavingne are the producers of this little show, with Bruno as the conductor providing direction from the orchestra pit.

Operas, when written, are often based on other written works. So for Bruno and Isabella to write an opera about the scandal in the theatre would have been unusual but not unheard of. But as a story it would be eminently suitable to have been transformed for the operatic stage.

Prior to Beethoven's composing, conductors weren't not required during an opera as there was no large orchestra to play the musical score. Small numbers to single musicians provided the accompaniment for early operas. Julio Mendez was a nod to this early phase of opera, and Bruno Wagner was a nod to what opera became.

About the Author

I was born in Macclesfield, Cheshire, UK, and raised in the nearby town of Wilmslow. From an early age, I discovered I had a flair and passion for writing.

I began writing at the age of 7 and was first published in 2010. I currently live with my partner, Matt, and our two cats in Christchurch, New Zealand.

As an avid horsewoman and gamer, I also have a passion for singing, dancing, the theatre, and my garden.

Facebook: https://www.facebook.com/AuthorC.S.Woolley

Instagram: https://www.instagram.com/thecswoolley

Website: http://cswoolley.com

TikTok: https://www.tiktok.com/@c.s.woolley.books

Acknowledgements

Writing can be an extremely lonely profession at times, but thankfully I never have to go through any of the pressures alone. My wonderful Matthew has been a source of constant support to me during all of my writing endeavours since we first met. I couldn't ask for a more fitting partner to share my life or love with.

Writing is not something I stumbled into either, my mother, Helen, took me, and my sisters, to the library every weekend when we were young to get different books, and I always maxed out the number of books I could get. Not only did she encourage me to read, but to write as well. To say I have been writing stories and poetry since I was 7 is not an exaggeration and the development of my writing career is due in no small part to her.

My mother-in-law, Lesley, has also been a source of

unflinching and unwavering support, something I could not

do without.

To Laura and Sam, who have read and offered opinions,

death threats and encouragement on my early drafts, you are

true treasures. Amy, you too are worth your weight and more

in gold for all your love and support.

It may seem that writers only function alone, but I am blessed

to be part of an amazing community of authors whom I know

who have helped push me to even greater heights and

success. For the last few months I have relied on a small

group of friends more than most, my dearest Victoria Tait,

Glenn Salter, Jacqui Penn, Theresa Papa, and Chez Churton,

my dear friends, thank you.

To Vicky, Ellie, Holly, Hollie, Frankel, Mags, Jordan Rex, and

Steve, you guys are an amazing source of support and I love you all.

To my amazing PA, Jordan, and to Holly, who joined our team this year, you are both incredible. I have no idea how I lived without you before you came into my life as I certainly could not live without you now. In these last few months of flux and life changes, you have been just amazing and I know that you have made everything that is to come possible!

And finally, to you, dear reader, without you there would be no books, no series, no career. I want to thank you for all the time that you spend reading my work, reviewing it, and sharing it with your friends and family. Without you, there would be nothing. Thank you from the bottom of my heart.

Until we meet again in my next book, thank you and adieu.

www.ingramcontent.com/pod-product-compliance
Lightning Source LLC
Chambersburg PA
CBHW011324310726
48973CB00011B/3046